A TEST OF SKILL

Where would Walking Toad be waiting for him? Not at the patch of woods, Morgan thought. Too far, too obvious. He searched again and spotted a ravine that paralleled the angle of the trail Walking Toad had been using. Doubled back and set up an ambush. Figured.

Morgan crouched and ran to the ditch through the flat land. He bent over and moved forward, his six-gun out, cocked and ready to fire. The ditch took a turn and as Morgan came to it he edged forward and looked around.

Twenty feet ahead, looking out on the trail where Morgan should have been, stood Walking Toad. He had an arrow nocked and ready. Morgan moved Indian-quiet. The redskin was concentrating on the trail and had his back turned. When Morgan was ten feet away he fired a shot into the dirt a foot from the Indian's shoulder.

Walking Toad jumped as if the shot had hit him. He turned slowly, anger clouding his face.

"Slide the arrows to me," Morgan said. "Now go up the bank slowly. I wouldn't want to have to wound you. I need this job."

APACHE RIFLES

28

BUCKSKIN

KIT DALTON

LEISURE BOOKS   NEW YORK CITY

A LEISURE BOOK®

April 1990

Published by

Dorchester Publishing Co., Inc.
276 Fifth Avenue
New York, NY 10001

Printed in the United States of America.

Chapter One

Lee Morgan saw the first coming, but he couldn't duck or dodge it. The knuckles met the side of his jaw and slammed him to the side. He dropped his own hands to catch his balance and another blow powered in, a short, right cross that jolted him to the floor on the seat of his pants.

The big Swede who had floored Morgan snorted and scowled down at him. "You want some more, Big Talker, you just get up on your feet."

Morgan pushed up with his hands and stood, weaving a little. The whole bar seemed blurred and misty, but the man in front of him was plain enough. He was two-inches taller than Morgan and at least thirty pounds heavier, all bone and muscle, with a lot of skill in bare knuckle fighting.

The Swede lunged forward and Morgan threw out a pair of jabs that bounced off the man's iron jaw and let him get in close enough to plow one fist into Morgan's belly, doubling him over for the uppercut that slammed on the point of Morgan's unprotected chin and lifted him straight for just a minute, then dropped him unconscious on the floor.

Morgan came to almost at once but everything was hazy and blurred and painful. His whole body hurt. The barkeep bent over him.

"Hey, Morgan, you all right? You want me to get the doc?"

Morgan shook his head. "Fine," he said through swollen lips. "I'm just fine and dandy like I was at a goddamned Sunday School picnic, can't you tell?"

The apron laughed. "Yeah, I guess you are okay. In that case, get the hell out of my saloon. Told you not to cadge drinks off my customers. You walk out, or want me to pitch you out with your face scooping up horse turds?"

Morgan pushed up to his feet, swayed a minute and reached out to the apron for support. Then his head cleared and he saw the front door. He struggled toward it. The first step was the worst, then it got easier and he moved at a drunk's overly cautious pace touching the wall only once for support.

The cloudy noontime fresh air revived him somewhat. He found a bench in front of the hardware store next to the saloon and eased down on it. He leaned his head back against the clapboards sucking in air to his starving lungs.

Offhand, Morgan couldn't remember when he had been bested so bad in a fist fight. Five years at least. He checked his holster. His six-gun was still there. He'd sold his rifle that morning for $10 to pay for last night's room, a big dinner and a bottle of whiskey. Now he didn't remember where the whiskey or the rest of his money had gone.

Damn!

He had his horse in the livery. Or did he sell her,

too? No, she was still there. A horse and a six-gun, a blanket and a small carpetbag containing the remainder of everything he owned. That was everything he had in the world. Gone was the Spade Bit Ranch in Idaho. Gone was the bank account in Denver and Boise. Every damn thing . . . gone.

Lee Buckskin Morgan closed his eyes and let out a long sigh. He couldn't remember ever being this down. Well, maybe that one time up by Seattle when he'd worked in that hardware store so he wouldn't starve or freeze to death. That was down.

This was down. He'd got word that there was a job waiting for him in Phoenix, a protection job for an important man who had been threatened. By the time Morgan arrived, the man decided he didn't need that kind of protection anymore. He paid Morgan's train fare and dismissed him. The next evening the man was shot to death in his own bed—but not by Morgan.

Word was out he was in Arizona and a banker in Yuma sent him a note and he rode over there. He had dinner, courtesy of the banker, and met two men who would work with him. That was when he found out that it was a straight killing job. A man had wronged the banker years before and now was a big rancher in New Mexico. It was a three man wipe out mission.

Morgan told the banker he wasn't that desperate and walked out. The other two gunslingers came after him intending to silence him, only to find that their draw was a little slow. Morgan shot one man in the shoulder and kicked the weapon out of the second one's hand.

That was just before the banker slammed his own six-gun down on Morgan's head. He found himself at the edge of Yuma with his horse and his blanket and small carpetbag. In his wallet where he'd had

$200 was a note telling him that if he ever came back to Yuma, he'd wind up in a deep grave on Boot Hill.

Being a prudent man, Morgan rode for Tucson. He had a friend there who might help him. Tucson was only about 65 miles from Tombstone. That was where the sheriff had put out a wanted poster on him a few years back. He hoped all of the papers had been lost or destroyed by now. It was bad paper.

When he left Tombstone that year the sheriff had cleared him of any fault in the death. It had been a fair fight, and Potts had even drawn first. But then the district attorney returned to town and discovered that his brother, Wilfred Potts, was dead. He filed the complaint and drew up the poster and now Morgan was wanted dead or alive for a $2,000 reward.

In a country where the average spread paid cowboys $25 and food a month, or $300 a year in wages, and a store clerk drew down about $400 a year, $2,000 was five years' wages. That poster had caused Morgan no end of problems from Seattle to Missouri.

Maybe the district attorney down there was out of office by now and the sheriff was new. It had all happened over six or seven years ago.

The trip to Tucson had turned out to be all risk of being so close to Tombstone and no benefit, he discovered. His friend had died of the pox a year before. Now he was without cash, and his rifle gone, and two saloon aprons had booted him out for sampling the free lunch without buying a beer.

Hell, it was getting toward roundup time. Maybe he could find a spot on one of the ranches as a straight rider. A top hand could almost always get a job during roundup.

Two men walked by slowly, talking. Morgan couldn't help but hear. They stopped near the hardware entrance.

"Damnation, Wilbur, I know it sounds good, but who wants to wander all over them deserts up in there? So they pay two-dollars a day, you stand a good chance of yourself getting killed or maybe even scalped."

The other man shook his head. "Hell, it would be fun. I know part of that country. Indians don't bother me none. I seen me a Chiricahua before."

Morgan kept his eyes closed. He'd heard it before. Two-dollars a day? He could use some of that work. But the Chiricahua?

"Big brother, you are crazy. You got to ride all the way north to the San Carlos Indian Reservation just to find out if they have enough scouts."

"Hell, three days at the most. Maybe ninety miles."

"Then you got to convince the army that you know enough about the area and about scouting that you can track them damn Indians through the desert."

"The story in the paper said they was hunting six scouts to go on a big push with the army, so I'm going. You don't want to come with me, fine."

The taller man grumbled. "You just think you're going. You got to tell Martha first, and she'll scratch your nose bloody, you wait and see."

The men went into the hardware and Morgan moved slightly on the bench, feeling the new bruises and some of the old ones. His body must look like a half-blue, half-white man by now.

Sixty dollars a month and food. Might do for a spell. It was the third time he'd heard about the army hiring scouts. Three times couldn't be just smoke in the wind.

First he'd have to ride 90 miles. Tough without any food. He sighed and stood. An involuntary groan seeped from his lips as he came erect. Damnation, he hated getting beat up in a fist fight. Hated losing and hated all the bruises and skinned knuckles and maybe a loose tooth or a black eye.

Morgan walked with only a slight limp as he went down half a block to the gunsmith. When Morgan went inside, the small man with round wire framed spectacles and almost no hair looked up and laughed softly.

"Morgan, figured you'd be back. Hey, you put up a good friend against Lars, I heard. Hard man to beat. Nobody has whipped him in over a year now. He's a bit touchy about anybody saying they have. I figured you're here to see what that Colt is worth."

Morgan unbuckled the gun belt and slid in on the wooden counter with the Colt in place.

"Whole thing. Gun and belt. They fit together nicely."

The gunsmith drew the revolver out of leather, emptied the rounds from the cylinder and then quickly examined the weapon with gentle hands.

"Nice piece, well cared for." He looked up. "Since you're a regular customer, I can give you $6 for the iron and $1 more for the leather. Best I can do."

"Done," Morgan said.

"Paper alright?"

"Whatever you've got, I won't have it long."

Morgan took the seven one-dollar greenbacks and stuffed them in his pocket. Outside he walked down to the general store. He moved with purpose now. Gone was the shuffle and the limp. Morgan pushed open the door to the general store and went back to the food section.

He chose carefully. It was more like a hundred miles to San Carlos reservation. Three days on the road. He knew exactly what he wanted to buy. Two tins of baked beans, two unsliced loaves of country bread, one jar of strawberry jam, a handful of beef jerky strips and a pound of cheddar cheese. He at last found a well used half gallon canteen. He wasn't that sure of water holes in this stretch of Arizona Territory.

Morgan grinned, feeling better than he had in weeks. "Watch out U.S. Army, here I come," he said as he wrapped his food in a gunny sack. He waved at the store owner and headed down the boardwalk toward his horse. It wasn't noon yet, he'd be able to get a ways north before dark.

He saw the two men coming toward him and veered to the outside of the boardwalk. They made the same move.

"Morgan, Lee Morgan?" one of the men rasped watching Morgan closely, his hand ready over his gun butt.

Morgan stopped. The two were of a kind, raw and trail dirty, right hands held low next to well used six-guns. Bounty hunters.

"What?" Morgan asked. "You gents speaking to me?"

"Yeah, speaking to you. Since you're Lee Buckskin Morgan we're damn well talking at you."

"Who? Morgan. Sorry you got the wrong man. My name is Amos Jerrico and I'm heading north."

"Only place you're heading, Morgan, is to the sheriff's office. He's got the paper on you. Won't do you no good to deny that you're Morgan. I'm from Tombstone. I was there the day you gunned down Winfred Potts in cold blood."

"I beg your pardon. I told you my name. Now if you'll excuse me, I have a trail to get moving along."

"Well now, he is denying it. He don't even have a six-gun the way he did in Tombstone. How do you suppose a feller like him is going to argue with two revolvers spitting out hot lead? Way I remember the poster, it said dead or alive."

Morgan moved up slowly. "Really, you must be mistaken. I admit I have a face that looks like a lot of other folks, but it's the first time I've been mistaken for a killer." He was within arm's reach of the two.

He bowed slightly and smiled. "Now, I'm sure you gents have figured out your mistake, so if you'll stand aside, I'm a little late."

One man laughed. He threw back his head and roared. That was when Morgan lashed upward with his right foot, his boot striking the laugher squarely in the crotch, crushing one testicle and jolting such pain through his system that the man was on his way to the boardwalk in a half second.

Even as his boot crushed the other man, Morgan's sack full of food and tins of beans slammed forward, striking the second man in the side of the head, driving him sideways and taking any fight out of him that might have been there.

Morgan kicked the second man's feet from under him and slid the six-gun from the attacker's holster as he fell.

By the time the crotch-kicked man could bellow out his pain, Morgan had slipped his iron from leather as well and now held both the guns with the two bounty hunters on the boardwalk.

The more slender man looked about Morgan's waist size.

"You, Big Mouth. Unbuckle that gunbelt and hand it up here before I do a little target practice on your ugly face."

The uninjured man swore softly. He shook his head in disgust with his own performance, opened the belt and handed it up to Morgan. A moment later it fit snugly around Morgan's waist. He put one of the six-guns in place and held the other. Then Morgan picked up his sack of foodstuff, thankful for the three tins of beans and their effect on the bounty man.

"I'm not sure who you gents were looking for, but that search is over. I don't enjoy being hassled by a couple of second rate bounty hunters, no matter how polite they might be. I'd suggest that you get your friend here over to the doc's office and see what he can do for the man's family jewels. My guess is that they are busted up some.

"If I see either of you again, I'll go for iron and let hot lead do my talking. Now get this trash off the city's boardwalk."

Morgan watched them as the unhurt man helped the other one to his feet, then limp away toward the doctor's office. Neither of them even looked behind at the easy mark they thought they had found.

Lee Buckskin Morgan chuckled as he watched them go. Then he jogged down the street to his horse, tied on the food behind his saddle and rode out of town to the north. He knew the way. He hadn't been through here for a few years, but that kind of high dry country didn't change much.

As long as he held due north and kept between Black Mountain on the left and Table Mountain on the right, he'd be fine. The more he thought of it as he rode out of town, the more he figured it would be a better route to cut toward Table Mountain and find the San Pedro River, which emptied into the Gila River, which ran about ten miles south of San Carlos headquarters. The river route would give him an easy way through the dry Arizona hills and mountains.

Morgan slapped the strongly built dun mare on the neck and she lifted to an easy canter and

Morgan grinned. "Dammit, U.S. Army, I hope you're ready for Lee Morgan. If I sign on to do some duty with you, I won't be like most other army scouts, you can depend on that!"

Chapter Two

It took Lee Morgan four days to ride to the army post near the headquarters of the Indian reservation at San Carlos. Halfway there, he told himself that there was only one way of life lower than scouting for the army, and that was begging. He'd done his share of begging this past month, he might as well climb up one rung and give the army one more go-round.

He'd scouted for Major Johnson in Montana for two months once, and left on not the best of terms. But the job had bridged him over a tough period.

Now with the army supposedly on a big push to polish off the Chiricahuas and especially Geronimo, the U.S. Army might stand him in good stead again.

He rode into the army camp about noon on the fourth day out of Tucson. There was no stockade around the place, just a loose group of buildings in the process of going up. A sentry told him where the fort's Commanding Officer was and he tied up at a rail outside the one story building and stamped the trail dust off his boots and pants and brushed some off his shirt.

Inside he found the usual corporal and sergeant major who glared at him like he was dog meat.

"Yeah?" the sergeant brayed.

"Hear you're looking for scouts who know the Chiricahua and their range and the Arizona-New Mexico border area in particular. I do."

The sergeant calmed himself. "Yeah, good, we're still short. You got a name?"

"Lee Morgan."

The sergeant looked up sharply. "Heard that name before, should I know you?"

"Not unless you're from Idaho or I sold you some lame horses."

"Must be some other hombre. Come on, the major will want to talk to you."

The sergeant knocked on one of two doors opening off the room and then pushed the panel open. He stepped in and left the way clear for Morgan.

"Major Phelps, I've got another candidate for scout. When would you like to see him?"

"By damn, right now. Send him in."

Morgan heard the exchange and he cringed. Another bombastic, self-important, army major. He'd had enough of those, but looked like he might have a new one.

The sergeant came out, waved Morgan inside and closed the door behind him.

Morgan took in the office in a glance. The usual. U.S. flag tacked to the wall, picture of the president, a Table of Organization of this army unit on the far wall with many changes on it, and a big, much used desk near the far window with a man standing behind it.

"Major, I'm Lee Morgan. Hear you need some scouts."

Major Phelps did not offer to shake hands. He stood so Morgan had to look at him against the light of the window. Morgan figured he was about five-ten, square built, with a moustache and no beard. He wore a new, just pressed uniform.

The major nodded and sat down, then Morgan could see his face. Slightly puffy and a little red from wind and sun, dark eyes and brows, hair almost black. The man's mouth was thin lipped and held tightly closed. He nodded.

"Morgan, I'm Major Phelps. In two days, I'm leaving this post and taking a thousand troops in a sweep against the damn Chiricahua. If we can rope in Geronimo, so much the better." He stood and went to a small scale wall map that showed the San Carlos reservation at the bottom and stretched upward and to the New Mexico border on the right.

"You know anything about the San Francisco and Blue Rivers?"

"Yes, sir. Over near the border. Run up into the San Francisco Mountains which are mostly in New Mexico."

The major looked surprised.

"Right. The Chiricahua. How do you slip up on them in their camp?"

"You don't. Usually, the first time you see a Chiricahua is five seconds before he kills you. They have the best system of lookouts and scouts I've ever seen. They live in dangerous country and had to become twice as deadly as the land to survive. You might beat them by running to ground their women and children, but cavalry will never outrun a Chiricahua brave on foot in his own territory."

"That we'll put to the test, Morgan. Can you sign?"

Morgan quickly signed, "Yes," then asked the major: "Are you a dog?" in the universal Indian sign language that was best known in the plains where it developed.

The major grunted. "I don't read sign too good. Also, I don't buy a pig in a poke, Morgan. The pay is $2 a day, but first I want to find out if you can track. Tell Sergeant Hines to set up the usual tracking test. That's all, Morgan. The sergeant will take care of you."

Morgan nodded. He wasn't about to salute and turned and walked out the door. Sergeant Hines looked up.

"Major says you're to set up the usual tracking test but I hope it isn't before I get to eat."

"A freeloader, huh?"

"Army business, army chow."

The army food was served by the headquarters company cook and wasn't much to brag about. They had poiled potatoes, bread, coffee and beef jerky which had been boiled and faintly resembled beef. The army still held a company cook responsible for food served in the barracks and camps.

"You came on a good day," Sergeant Hines said. "Usually, we don't eat this well." He pointed the way and they walked to the edge of the camp where an assortment of Indian wickiups huddled around the banks of a small stream.

Two men came forward. Both were small, Apache of some band, about five-foot three. Buckskin did not sign a greeting to them, since the less they knew about him right now the better.

"This is Elk Leg, a Coyotero Apache," Sergeant Major Hines said pointing at the younger man. "His brother, Walking Toad." The men nodded. "I have a new candidate for your tracking test. Don't make it too hard, we have only four White Eye scouts and the major wants six."

Both Indians nodded.

"This is the exercise," the sergeant explained. "Both these Apaches will leave here and go out two miles into the countryside. Your job is to track them. Both will be on foot since the Apache would rather walk and run than ride.. You can use your own horse or I'll furnish you with one.

"If you find them out two miles, one will go out another two miles on foot, and you can track him either on foot or on your mount. At the far point an army canteen will be left with certain markings on it. Your job is to find it and return it to my office as quickly as you can."

"Will both these Indians be at the two mile point when I get there?" Morgan asked.

The sergeant shrugged. "That's up to them. Your job is to bring back that canteen. We'll start the trail at the back of the fort headquarters building."

The Indians both nodded and ran into a wickiup and came out with an army canteen. Each had a knife and a bow and three arrows. The Indians walked beside them toward the fort.

"By the time we get back to the headquarters and get your horse ready, the two Coyoteros will have a half hour start," Sergeant Hines said. "That's our usual lead since this country is so barren and flat."

At the headquarters, Morgan took a long drink of water and chewed on some jerky from his pack. He left everything on his horse. If he unloaded his gear here it probably would vanish before he got back. Morgan rested in the shade of the front overhang of the building until the sergeant came out and nodded.

"They have a half hour head start. Good luck, Morgan. We need another man who knows an Apache footprint from a tree toad."

Morgan rode around the building and stepped down from his mount. He saw nothing at first. He rode out 50 yards and began a semicircle around the headquarters building. Not even an Apache could cross this kind of desert dry land without leaving some sign.

He found it about halfway around. At least one of the Coyoteros had headed due east toward the Gila Mountains. The land was semi-desert with maybe four or five inches of rainfall a year. He found where a moccasined foot had crushed a clump of bunch grass and half of the stems had not yet worked back up to their normal position.

A step ahead of that he saw where toes had dug into the sand as the man walked rapidly. Morgan walked along leading his dun mare. Twenty feet later he found the second set of prints coming in from the side. Now both sets moved steadily eastward. Ahead he could see a brush line, maybe two miles away. That's when he remembered that the San Carlos creek headed up this way.

The scuffs and bent weeds and toe scuffs turned sharply to the left and angled into a draw. The watercourse had been dug out little by little as maybe one or two rains a year contributed to a runoff that would gouge out more dirt and rocks and sand and push it downstream.

Soon the barranca was deep enough to hide a man. The prints continued for a quarter of a mile. The Coyotero Apaches were trotting now, that Indian trot that can eat up six to seven miles an hour and that they can sustain for six hours without a break.

A hundred yards ahead they came to a place where the draw cut through slab rock. It was a broad sheet twenty yards wide. Morgan nodded and ran to the side of the draw and checked the dirt along the two foot bank. He found nothing.

On the other side of the draw where the slab rock vanished under six feet of top dirt and stones, he found where the two Indians had stepped carefully up the bank and then crouched as they moved forward slowly.

They must have been in view of him by then. He led the horse up the bank then trailed the Apaches down a slight incline to another arroyo heading at a 30 degree angle to the first one and more to the east.

Ten minutes later he came to a sparse ribbon of trees that followed a three-inch deep and ten-foot wide San Carlos creek. On the bank with his feet in the water sat one of the Apaches. He turned, seemed surprised and waved. It was Elk Leg.

The Coyotero Apache grinned. "Make brother work," he said. "You much fast."

"You really weren't trying to lose me," Morgan said. "No circles, no cutbacks, no hidden trails."

The Indian shrugged. "Low pay, low work." He laughed. "Now, you find brother Toad. He slippery."

Morgan looked at the water. The Indian would probably go upstream since downstream would take them back too near the fort in two miles. He would walk in the water to wipe out his prints.

Morgan stepped into the saddle and moved upstream on the near side, leaning down from the saddle watching the ground along the bank. He didn't expect to find any wet marks, but there would be an indication when the Coyotero left the water. Would it be on this side or the other?

"The other side," he said out loud and worked his mount across the hock deep water. On the far side, he rode upstream again checking the shoreline, being especially watchful where the brush was thick. It would be a fine spot to come out and not leave any tracks near the shore.

He moved a quarter of a mile and found nothing. Maybe it was the other side. Maybe the Indian took the simplest way. He wasn't getting paid any less for a sloppy job.

Morgan decided to give it another five minutes. Just before he was set to move across the creek, he spotted bent over grass and a broken branch on the edge of some brush next to the creek. He got down and studied it carefully. Two moccasin prints showed at the edge of the brush, then another one where the Indian had stepped directly on the fresh dirt thrown out of a squirrel hole. On east.

Now as Morgan watched the trail again, walking, he could see the sign six or eight yards ahead. He began to trot, emulating the Apache, but after a half mile he lost the tracks.

Crossing. He waded through the ankle deep water to the other side of the ten-foot wide creek and almost at once found the prints, but now instead of keeping to the easterly direction, the tracks turned what he guessed was due north.

About a half mile in that direction he saw a clump of trees. The obvious destination. But not this time. Walking Toad would be somewhere else. Morgan moved out cautiously. The trail was too easy. Scuffs, toe marks, a broken desert flower, a kicked aside cactus branch that had lain in the same spot perhaps for years.

For the first time, Morgan wondered why the two Indians had started out with their bows and arrows. Why? To make the search more realistic? Maybe to shoot a stray rabbit for the stew pot? No. Then he remembered the arrows. They did not have hunting points on them. As near as he could remember, the arrows had flat, long slabs of rock similar to an arrow head, but perhaps tied in place only for weight.

Yes! The Indians must have orders to ambush him, to fire their blunted arrows and claim any hits. Morgan dropped to the ground. He left the horse tied to a hefty greasewood plant and moved out 20 yards in a crouch, then lifted up and studied the surrounding territory.

Almost flat. Here and there a shallow water course heading generally back toward the San Carlos. Where would Walking Toad be waiting for him? Not at the patch of woods. Too far, too obvious. He searched again and spotted a ravine that paralleled the angle of the trail Walking Toad had been using. Doubled back and set up an ambush. Figured.

The arroyo was 20 yards to the left of the trail. Morgan crouched and ran to the ditch through the flat land. He dropped into it where it was only three-feet deep but it sank lower ahead.

He bent over again and moved forward, his six-gun out, cocked and ready to fire. The gully deepened gradually and another 40 yards ahead was low enough so he could stand up and be out of sight. The ditch took a turn another 20 yards ahead and as Morgan came to it he edged forward and looked around.

Twenty feet ahead, looking out on the trail where Morgan should have been, stood Walking Toad. He had an arrow nocked and ready. Morgan moved Indian-quiet. The redskin was concentrating on the trail and had his back turned. When Morgan was ten feet away he fired a shot into the dirt a foot from the Indian's shoulder.

Walking Toad jumped as if the shot had hit him. He turned slowly, anger clouding his face.

"Slide the three arrows to me," Morgan said. The Indian did so. The big Colt revolver's muzzle never stopped pointing at the Indian target.

"Now go up the bank slowly. I wouldn't want to have to wound you. I need this damn job."

A half hour later, Morgan cantered up to the front door of the Fort Commander's office. Walking Toad had his hands tied behind his back and a lariat noose around his throat as he trotted along beside the dun.

A shout went up and six men scrambled out the fort headquarters door. Sergeant Hines was in front.

"I'll be damned," Sergeant Hines said. "Nobody ever got out of that trap before."

Morgan looped the lariat over his saddlehorn and stepped down. He took the noose off the Indian's neck and cut the rawhide from his hands. Then Morgan gave Walking Toad his bow and three arrows.

"Me damn pissed," Walking Toad said. He shook his head. "Hire, him damn good tracker, almost good enough to be Apache!"

Chapter Three

Major Phelps hired Morgan on the spot. There never was any canteen. The last dozen men who'd tracked the Apaches in the test had been "shot" with three arrows and taken back to the fort. Three of them had been hired anyway because they were good trackers.

Morgan was assigned to a barracks where the other trackers were quartered. One of them was drunk and had been for two days. The other two were playing poker with the soldiers using matches for counters because nobody had any money.

One of the three was a Mexican who spoke good English. Morgan practiced his Spanish for awhile, then got his gear from the supply sergeant. Regulations allowed him to wear whatever he wanted to but he had found out before that if he had a uniform on, he was less likely to be singled out as a target.

He took two pairs of blue pants and two shirts with no insignia on them. He chose to wear his own hat, but got two of the army neckerchiefs. They would come in handy. Right now he had no plans to turn the uniforms back in when he moved on to better employment. He also kept his own boots but got four pairs of army socks.

That afternoon, the major had the three sober scouts in for a briefing on the general area where they were going and what they hoped to accomplish.

He had placed some transparent tracing paper over the section of the map near the Blue and San Francisco Rivers and circled the points.

"Gentlemen, I'm a commander who wants my lead men to know what's going on, where we're marching, and what we hope to accomplish. These areas are the Blue and San Francisco Rivers. We have been led to believe that some of the recent uprisings and battles on the San Carlos reservation were caused in part by renegades who fled to the San Francisco Mountains.

"Indeed, more than 200 of the warriors from this agency have vanished and we believe they are in the mountains preparing for raids along the southern half of Arizona. Then they will flee into Mexico.

"Our job is to overtake them, engage them in battle before they can raid again, and destroy their ability to make war."

He looked around.

"How many men will you have, Major?" the Mexican man asked.

"A few more than a thousand. We'll be self contained with wagons, about half infantry and the rest well mounted cavalry. We have five troops of the Fourth Cavalry, two troops from the Sixth Cavalry. Speed will not be our purpose.

"The renegades have swept through several settlements and raided four ranches. They have horses. More than 20 dead whites have been reported.

"General Sherman has ordered us to end this

annual Apache uprising and he's promised to furnish us with as many men as we need." The major looked around. "Are there any more questions?"

"Do these renegades have women, children and their camping gear with them?" Morgan asked.

"Some do, and some don't. The women and children will slow them down. Our first job is to find them."

"I've heard they are heading for the rugged Peloncillo Mountains farther south," the other white guard said. "Will we track them in there?"

"We'll follow them wherever they go, even into Mexico. Remember, we have a treaty with Mexico for reciprocal crossing of each other's borders with armed troops. This is to facilitate just such a chase if the Apaches raid here and run to Mexico, or if they raid in Mexico and run back up here."

The major looked around and there were no more questions. "Those of you who brought mounts when you came will leave them here. You'll all have army mounts, saddles and equipment. That applies to rifles as well. I want all the scouts to have Spencer repeater carbines. You can bring your own revolvers if you wish. That's all. We'll be riding out the day after tomorrow. Morgan, I want you to remain. The rest of you are excused."

Morgan frowned slightly but kept his seat as the two other men left the room and closed the door.

"Morgan, you'll be my lead scout. I like bright men who can think on their feet. I also like scouts who know when they are about to be bushwacked by friendly or renegade Indians. You'll be with me leading the column or out in front.

"We'll be taking with us a small company of what we call 'scout troopers.' These are Apaches who can ride and form a self contained unit of 20 men we use for forward operations, a kind of stalking horse,

I guess you'd call them. Only one or two of these savages speak any English. You'll be riding with them from time to time, so it's good that you can sign.

"Oh, I want you to pick up a pair of field glasses from supply. Sergeant Hines will write you a chit for them. After that, you better pick out a mount and get tack and a saddle. We still have the McClellan in this unit. That's all, Morgan. Welcome aboard."

Lee looked for a horse for half the morning. Most of the mounts in this fort were browns and blacks. Some commanders wouldn't buy anything but a black.

At last, Morgan found a pen where some of the culls had been put. There was one flashy sorrel with a nearly white mane and tail, a true palomino. But it would stand out too much. He kept looking.

In the far side of the lot he found a buckskin. The mare was not large, maybe fourteen-and-a-half hands, but she was a light yellow almost sand color that would blend in well with the Arizona landscape. She had a deep chest and he liked the way she moved as he followed her around the corral. He put a rope on her and got a bridle, then grabbed her mane and jumped up on her bareback. She snorted once, then responded to the reins as he walked her around the corral. She moved like a fine ticking clock, precise, automatic. He rode her bareback to the tack room where the sergeant snorted when he saw her.

"Wait until you see her move," Morgan said.

They outfitted her with a McClellan saddle and Morgan looked for the saddlehorn, but there wasn't one. Cavalrymen didn't do much steer roping so they didn't need a horn to tie their rope to.

The buckskin stood motionless as they slipped the bridle in place, put on a saddle blanket and then the McClellan. She didn't blow up her belly when the cinch strap went around. By the time they got her saddled, the tack room sergeant had a much better feeling for the animal.

Morgan mounted and took her up and down in front of the tack room. She worked a canter so smooth he thought she was walking. The sergeant pushed the fatigue cap back on his head and scratched his thinning hair.

"Be damned. Now there is a fine mount. Just because she's a buckskin nobody wanted her."

Morgan grinned. "Thank the troops for me. Where do I put her, and my tack?"

The sergeant detailed a man to Morgan who showed him where to put his horse and the saddle and other gear. Morgan thanked him, then took the buckskin for a two mile ride around the outside of the fort to get used to her. They settled into a fine operating unit after a mile and Morgan was pleased with his army mount.

Back at his barracks for two more nights, Morgan met two more scouts. One was a Mexican man who spoke precise English, and the other one an Anglo. The drunk was starting to sober up. He had run out of money so he had no other choice. All of the men had been scouts for the army before, three of them in this area. Morgan started to memorize their names, then gave up. Some of them he might not see again. He'd learn the names of the men he would be working with.

One was younger than the rest. He was the Mexican lad with the precise English. The young man was no more than 22, Morgan guessed.

He held out his hand. "Hello, I'm Alfredo."

Morgan took his hand. "Hi, I'm Morgan. You've been in this country before."

"Yes. I was born here, actually, a little south of here, but I know the whole area."

"I'll come asking directions from you if I get lost, Alfredo."

They went over to the headquarters mess hall and had the evening meal—lots of salt pork and baked beans and boiled turnips. Morgan had no idea where the army bought turnips to issue to the troops. One thought lifted his spirits. Maybe if he rode with the Apache scout unit they would provide their own food. Apaches living off the land would do much better than salt pork and hardtack, he was sure.

Morgan was called to the major's office late the next day where a dozen officers stood around the map. A moment later the major came in and the men snapped to attention. Morgan watched with mild amusement. It had always struck him a little silly how junior officers snapped and became spit and polish when a higher ranking officer was around.

"At ease men, this is your final briefing before we hit the field in the morning. Boots and Saddles at six a.m. We will be moving out then.

"Now the background I promised you at our other meeting. I expect everyone of my field officers to know as much about the project, the mission, as I do. Here's what I know.

"This all goes back two years to Cibicu when Colonel Eugene A. Carr of the Sixth Cavalry was ordered to capture and arrest the medicine man, Nakaidoklini, in his village on Cibicu creek. He was captured without gunfire, then transported. The first night on the way back, his followers attacked the army unit and in the fight, the medicine man was killed.

"This riled up the hostiles and soon led to an attack by Apaches laying seige to Fort Apache where several men were killed and Colonel Carr's horse was shot out from under him.

"Most independent and warlike of all the six Apache tribes are the Chiricahuas and the Warm Springs. Many of them lived in Mexico and still do. Others were on a reservation 15 miles up the Gila from San Carlos.

"These are the tribes we are hunting today. They are the toughest of the Apaches, and while official and unofficial reports call these warriors 'renegades,' they are not. A renegade is an outlaw from his tribe or band. These warriors constitute the majority of the tribes and are fighting for their lives.

"As troops swarmed into the San Carlos reservation after the attack on Fort Apache, it caused rumbles in the Chiricahua camps. They had been living peacefully in their wickiups at the Camp Goodwin sub-agency. Now with all the military around, they got edgy and talked of going to Mexico.

"Late in the year, the Chiricahua took in some fleeing White Mountain Indians the army was chasing and that set off a general exodus by the Chiricahuas into the mountains and into Mexico.

"The Apache threat was again hovering over the Southwest. For a year, the Apaches were far to the south near the headquarters of the Gila River deep in a tangled mass of mountains and gullies in Mexico. Now they have crossed the border again and continue their raiding on richer targets. Our job is to rout them out of their stronghold, punish them, reduce them by arms so they never again can function as a hostile force."

"Sir, does that mean we wipe them out to a man?" a captain asked.

The major smiled. "Captain, we engage them in a military operation and attempt a complete victory."

The officers chuckled. They had heard double talk by their leaders before, saying one thing, meaning another.

"Gentlemen, I'd like you to meet our head scout, Lee Morgan. He's demonstrated that he can track a flea across an elephant's back, and can slip up and capture an Apache in the open desert when the Apache knows he's coming. Take a bow, Morgan, it may be your last chance."

Morgan walked forward, waved his hat and then moved to the back of the room again.

"Gentlemen, are there any questions?"

"How far are we moving a day? My infantry isn't good for much over 20 miles."

"Lieutenant, we've set our daily march at just under 20 miles. In the early phases we are in no hurry. You realize a band of Apaches can make six miles an hour on foot, cover 60 miles a day and be ready to fight?"

"I've heard that, Major Phelps. I've never had the chance to fight any of them after their 60 mile trip."

"Pray to God that you will this time, Lieutenant."

The group chuckled again.

The major looked around. "If there are no more questions, that will be all."

The officers snapped to attention, turned and left the room. Morgan was in front of them all.

In the barracks that night he and the rest of the scouts made last minute preparations. Someone treated them to a cold bottle of beer each and then they put their small packs and saddlebags in order, ready to roll the blanket with a spare uniform inside and get to their mounts at 5:15 A.M.

"Once more into the fray to fill up the breach with our bodies," one of the scouts said. He laughed. "Let's hope it doesn't come to that. You know what happened during the Charge of the Light Brigade." He looked around. "It got its ass whipped. Wiped out to a man, as I remember."

On that happy note the scouts turned in. It would be the last bunk with a mattress they would see for a long time.

Chapter Four

The next three days were everything Morgan disliked about being a scout for the army. The only good part was that he had not signed on for any definite stay. His employment could be terminated by either party at a moment's notice, which suited Morgan just fine.

They had just endured three days of slogging along across the desert-dry Natanes Plateau. He had no idea how the government expected the Indians to make a living off this dry, brittle, baked desert that formed a huge section of the San Carlos Indian Reservations.

The cavalry riders had it easy. A 40 mile day would be more normal for them. The foot soldiers bitched and screeched in anger, but underlying it all was the fact that every one of them had volunteered for the army.

They came to Eagle Creek after four in the afternoon of the third day. This was one of the small streams that ran into the San Francisco River. They were about ten degrees off Mitchell Peak, an 8,000 footer that poked sullen and barren up toward the southern end of the San Francisco range.

So far the troops had traveled in one long column, mounted men four abreast and foot soldiers also four abreast. The wagons were put out 50 yards so they wouldn't throw up too much dust for the troops to eat. In this case, Major Phelps and his scout led the column with the foot sloggers next and the mounted troops bringing up the rear again for dusty reasons. Four hundred horses throw up a cloud of dust that's hard to imagine if you haven't ridden through one. Morgan had, more than once, when riding drag on a trail drive of 2,000 cattle. That's 8,000 hooves pounding the ground into powder fine dust that lifts and swirls on even the faintest of breezes.

They stopped at the creek, watered the horses and planned their strategy. They would split into two groups, each with half the infantry and cavalry. They would drive east over the ridge, past Mitchell Peak until they came to the San Francisco River. They should be somewhere near the confluence with the Blue.

Half the troops would charge up the Blue searching out any hostiles they might find. The other half of the party would work upstream on the San Francisco River where the water volume was reduced until no sizeable band of Indians could camp on it.

If the enemy was found, they would be engaged with special attention to killing the warriors and letting the women and children go free. With no warriors to hunt for them, the women and children would be forced to march back to the reservation for sustenance.

The column reached one of the streams an hour before darkness and Major Phelps called Morgan.

"Work up this crick for as far as necessary to find out if this is the San Francisco or the Blue. The Blue feeds into this one, but are we above or below the confluence?"

Morgan nodded and kicked his buckskin into motion. He went alone working through the thin shield of brush along the stream. Most of the mountains and ridges here were bare, rocky, wind blown and sun baked. Not enough rain came to keep the slopes green and the runoff needed to feed this small stream had to come from a surprisingly large area. But the small ribbon of green was enough to hide and sustain a band of Chiricahuas.

Morgan moved the buckskin gently along the stream, walking, cantering when the area opened up. He wanted to find the junction before dark, if he could. From what he remembered of the map, the mountain they had just come around lay almost due west of the junction of the two streams. Two miles, maybe three at the most.

It turned out to be about four. He sat in heavy brush and saw where the Blue came in from the north. So they were downstream on the San Francisco. Morgan was about to turn the mare around when two Indian hunters burst from some brush 100 yards ahead, fired arrows and then one gave a cry of victory as his arrow dropped some small animal, probably a rabbit.

Morgan grabbed his mare's nostrils so she wouldn't make horse talk at the strangers. The Indian hunters picked up their kill and hurried back into the woods and vanished upstream.

Morgan turned his mount around and rode at the best speed he could down the stream to the camp of 1,000 U.S. Army troopers and cavalry.

He found the major eating his supper in his Sibley tent. The conical tent had been carried on the first supply wagon and was quickly set up for the major. He shared it with the ranking captain who would lead the second half of the unit. The rest of the officers were not allowed to bring their tents, but each had an orderly to cook food from his private supply.

Major Phelps put down a leg and thigh of a jackrabbit and looked up at Morgan.

"Yes?"

"We're on the San Francisco, sir. The Blue is about four miles ahead. I also saw two Indians shooting a jack rabbit with bow and arrow. I was too far away to identify them. They took their catch and went upstream on the Blue."

"Goddamn, did I find the best Scout in the southwest, or didn't I? Damn good work, Morgan." He paused a minute. "You eaten anything yet? Come and join us. Captain Casemore and I have more than we can eat. Besides, you're going to need it."

"I'll eat with the men, sir."

"Don't think so. Time for fires is over. Unless you want to eat cold salt pork. Come on, we need to talk."

Morgan looked at the half a jack rabbit still on a platter. It had been roasted over a fire on an iron skewer. He took off his hat and sat down near the low table.

"Eat your fill, cause I have a night mission for you. Want you to take Gimpy, he's the Apache scout we have with the bed leg. You and Gimpy go up the Blue and find out just where them hostiles have their camp. How far would you think it might be?"

Morgan had eaten half the leg and thigh piece. He finished chewing and looked up. "These two I saw were short range hunters. They had no pemmican roll, so they wouldn't get more than six to eight miles from their camp. They could be camped from ten to twelve miles from here."

"Goddamn, we might be lucky first shot out of the chute here, Casemore."

The captain passed Morgan a thick slab of bread. It wasn't army bread. Some squaw had baked it in her funny little oven. There was butter, too, and Morgan lifted his brows in surprise.

"Just don't tell the troops how well we're eating," Major Phelps said. "This won't last for long, and then we'll be back to tinned beans and corned beef and at last the hardtack and salt pork the troops eat."

Captain Casemore groaned. "Damn right. This is just a short term compensation for being in this ridiculous country. Why anyone would want to live in Arizona or New Mexico is beyond me."

Morgan ate another piece of rabbit, a part of the back or ribs, he wasn't sure. It had more meat on it than he had seen in a week. Now if he had a good cold beer he could sleep until noon tomorrow.

"About the scouting mission, we'll work up the creek until we spot the camp. You want to know how many wickiups, about how many warriors, and if there are women and children?"

"Yes, and if they have horses. Some of the Chiricahuas have taken to riding horses, making them slipperier than a new bar of soap." He sipped at his coffee. Morgan took the chance and downed half the cup of coffee they had provided for him.

"Of course, we don't want you to alert any of them. They probably will have out lookouts and rear guards. If they do, go around them, don't kill them. That would alert the whole camp.

"We'll be ready to move out of here in time to

stage a dawn attack. If they're only 10 miles, we can sleep in longer. Get back as fast as you can."

Morgan nodded, took one more piece of the rabbit, his fourth, and stood. "I better see to my horse. I figure we'll ride as far as we can so we can get back faster. The final scout once we find their camp will be on foot, of course."

"Of course," Captain Casemore said with a touch of disdain.

Major Phelps called in his orderly and spoke to him. He hurried out.

"My orderly, Rodin, has gone to bring Gimpy. You tell him what you're up to. Be best if you can leave as soon as possible."

"Yep, think you're right," Morgan said, cutting through the military formalities. Captain Casemore looked up sharply, but Morgan ignored him. "Be back soon as possible," Morgan said and went out the flap of the Sibley tent grinning at the look on the Captain's face.

By the time he got his mount re-saddled, fed a ration of grain and well-watered, the Indian Scout Gimpy was at hand. He rode bareback on an army horse that seemed a little bit puzzled by the whole affair.

Morgan signed that they would go up the Blue stream to find a band of Indians camped there.

"Scout them out?" Gimpy asked.

"Right, and come back with our hair," Morgan said and both laughed.

They rode along the side of the San Francisco River out of the brush for the first four miles, then moved in when the Blue turned due north.

It was full dark now, and they moved at a slow walk through the brush and trees. Morgan took the lead. They rode as quietly as possible, and at last went to the outside of the brush again for a more silent approach. They had gone what Morgan estimated to be five miles up the Blue when Morgan held up his hand and both horses stopped.

Far ahead he heard dogs barking. "Dogs bad news," Morgan said to Gimpy who nodded. They went two more miles before Morgan sniffed the air and pointed. "Campfires," he signed.

They both got off their mounts, tied them to brush and moved forward. Morgan left his Spencer on the horse. He checked the hold down strap on his own Colt .45 and then they walked ahead without a sound. After 20 feet, Gimpy looked at Morgan.

"Are you Apache?" Gimpy signed.

"Buffalo Apache," Morgan signed back and the Apache grinned.

They moved another mile through the trees and grass along the stream. It had been getting smaller for a time, but now maintained its course and size. Always it came from the north.

Morgan judged the time. It had been about eight o'clock when he and Gimpy left. They had been gone more than an hour. It might be nine-thirty. Most of the Indians would be sitting around their cooking fires in wickiups if they had time, or sitting in front of a quickly built lean to.

If women and children were along it would be a softer, easier camp. But since they were on the run, they surely would have out security of some kind. Teenage boys on high places during the day to spot any travelers coming from afar. At night that would mean guards, lookouts, someone watching the outlying areas. They would not leave the river approach unprotected.

Who would be there? Where would he be? Go around an Apache? You come do it, Major Phelps.

Gimpy and Morgan had taken turns in the lead.

It meant the man behind could relax a little, rest a little. Now Gimpy stopped with one foot in the air. He pointed.

An Indian stepped to the edge of the water 30 feet ahead of them in a splash of moonlight, bent down and scooped up two handfuls and drank. When he finished he washed off his face with more water, shook himself dry and vanished back into the shadows along the far side of the stream.

Gimpy pointed back the way they had come.

When they had worked 40 yards to the rear and out of the brush, they changed directions again, but now climbed up the side of the small valley where the stream ran. There was scatterings of scrub pine on the hill, and here and there a splash of grease-wood. There was definitely more rainfall in this section.

They worked up the slope to the top and over the ridgeline, then followed north again toward what must be an Indian village or campsite.

It took them another half hour to spot the camp. It lay along the Blue, 300 yards below them in the valley that here had spread out to over 200 yards wide. The river ran on the far side where they counted 32 lean-tos in the moonlight.

"It does not look like renegades," Gimpy signed.

"Let's go look," Morgan signed back.

The two men moved down the barren slopes like ghost shadows, floating from one small bit of cover to the next, moving slowly, Apache style, when they had to cover a moonlit stretch of open ground. After half an hour, they were in the fringes of the brush along the creek, less than 30 feet from one lean-to. They had not seen nor heard a dog. Morgan figured what they heard before might have been some coyote dog crosses in the brush.

Gimpy looked around the lean-to. He held up his

hand for Morgan to wait and he made his way all around the shelter. He came back smiling.

"All men," he signed. "Not neat camp. No women. Three men in this lean-to."

At the north part of the camp they found the small herd of horses, ten or fifteen at the most. They would be used mostly for pulling travois to carry the men's belongings.

Gimpy signed "Now what do we do?"

Morgan signed quickly. "Go back."

It took them an hour to get back to their horses, then a half hour more of hard riding to reach the soldiers' camp. They got there just before midnight. Morgan went to the Sibley tent and had the major's orderly wake him up.

When Morgan finished his report, the Major lit a coal oil lamp and squinted at his map.

"So, you figure they're about ten miles up the Blue. They have a lookout more than a mile downstream from their camp. Unusual. These damn Apaches? Fourteen miles. We'll need you and Gimpy to lead off and go in to eliminate the lookout. Then we'll move in past you, position our troops and be ready for sunrise."

"Yes, sir. Any sense in my going to sleep?"

"We won't leave here until one o'clock."

"How many men you taking, Major?"

"How many? I figured all 500."

"It's a tight, close quarters situation, sir. Could I suggest you go with 120 cavalry. That way we can move in quicker, get positioned, and then ride down from both sides into the campsite. That little valley is 300 yards wide right there."

"Mmmmmm. How long is the camp? Thirty shelters, you say."

"Spread out for maybe 200 yards. Gimpy figured there are no women or children there, only warriors."

"Yes. Well, you've been on the ground. You and Gimpy say 90 warriors at the most?"

"Our estimate, yes, sir."

The major made his decision quickly. "All right, Morgan. I'll go along with your recommendation. That's why I hired you. You and Gimpy still have the forward lookout. We'll ride with 150 cavalrymen at 2:00 A.M. Have a nap. I'll see that you're awakened in time."

"Yes sir, Major Phelps. And thank you."

"What for, Morgan?"

"For the rabbit. Best damn meal I've had in a week."

Morgan found his blankets, spread them out next to some brush where he could hear the chatter of the small stream, and went to sleep.

Chapter Five

As it turned out, there was no need for Morgan and Gimpy to kill the lookout they had spotted a mile from the Chiricahua camp. On the way up the Blue river toward the camp, Major Phelps questioned Morgan again about the situation.

"You say the valley is about 300 yards wide, with the stream on the right as we're riding forward?"

"Yes, sir. The creek is hock deep, 10 feet wide, and where the camp is situated it's about 50 yards from the right hand side of the valley and 250 from the other side."

The lookout is how far from the camp?"

"At least a mile."

"No need to kill the lookout. Half of us will ride up on the back side of both ridgelines, you said they weren't too high. That way we can put 75 troopers on one flank and 75 men on the other and have a good crossfire down into the lean-tos as soon as it gets light. After a steady barrage of rifle fire, we can charge down with our pistols and finish them off."

"Sounds reasonable, Major. They have 15 to 20 horses at the north end of their camp. You might want to use a small blocking force of, say five men, at both ends of the camp near the river."

The major glanced up, irritated. "Who the hell is running this campaign, anyway, Morgan?"

Morgan smiled in the darkness but remained quiet.

"Damn, yes, yes. That's a good idea, I'll take care of it. When we get five miles upstream on the Blue River, we'll split our forces. I want you with me, and Gimpy will take the other half of the men under Captain Vincent."

"Yes, sir," Morgan said, still grinning.

"We both should arrive in position slightly before daylight. Then when we both are in place, the dawn will bring the attack."

"As you say, Major."

At the five mile point, the column stopped and the major divided his troops. Morgan signed to Gimpy what he was supposed to do, and Captain Vincent was instructed by Major Phelps. When he had finished signing, Morgan figured Gimpy knew what was to happen.

An hour later they were ready. Morgan was poised with the Major and half the troopers on the ridgeline to the left of the Chiricahua camp. They were spread out about five yards between men so they covered the length of the Apache camp. They had dismounted and lay with rifles pointing over the ridge at the camp barely visible below.

It was 15 or 20 minutes to dawn, perhaps a half hour.

Phelps walked up and stared at Morgan.

"Have you heard or seen anything of the other

men on the far ridge?"

"Nope."

"Give the signal. Strike one match and let it flare until it goes out."

Morgan tore a stinker match off a round packet from his pocket, struck it on his boot sole, and cupped it in his hand pointing it at the far ridge.

A moment later at match flared 300 yards away, and there was an easy to hear sigh on the Major's side of the valley. The trap was set. At dawn, Major Phelps would fire the first shot and they would begin the attack.

Morgan hadn't thought about it before, but suddenly he didn't want to have any part in the slaughter he figured was coming. He knew what would happen. He had been part of it, but at least he didn't have to fire at the Indians who would be trapped below. He couldn't help them, but at least he didn't have to kill any of them.

Major Phelps lay nearby, his Spencer cocked and ready. He watched the sky, then looked again at the shadows below that were the shelters of the Chiricahuas. He checked his pocket watch, studied the sky again.

Gradually, streaks of lighter shades pierced the eastern sky. Then the whole sky seemed to lighten all at once, and it was dawn.

"Get ready to fire, pass the word," the major said to the man on each side of him. The order went down to all the men on the western side of the valley. The major waited a few moments longer for the message to reach the end of the lines each way, then he lifted his rifle, sighted in on the center of the nearest lean-to, and fired.

The sharp, clear crack of the .52 caliber rifle round leaving the muzzle of the Spencer and slapping into the side of the shelter splashed like

a searing rocket through the early dawn stillness.
Then the little valley became a shooting gallery as
150 rifles fired.

At first, from below, there was a surprised, dazed
quiet. A warrior ran out of his lean-to and stepped
behind a tree as he fired a rifle at the western ridge.
To his deadly surprise, three rifle rounds jolted into
him from the east.

Then there was a pause in the firing as the
cavalrymen watched for specific Apache warrior
targets to aim at.

Four Chiricahua warriors broke from behind a
lean-to and darted north toward the horses. They
ran from tree to tree trying to get to their small
band of mounts at the north end of camp. None of
them made it.

Fewer than a handful of the hostiles below had
been shot when Major Phelps called to his bugler.
"Boots and Saddles call," he bellowed over the rifle
fire.

The bugle blared out the traditional call to get
into the saddle. Almost at once, the firing stopped
as the troopers moved to step into their saddles. At
that moment 20 Indians sensed the opening and
sprinted from their shelters toward the deeper
brush covering around the stream.

When the firing had started, Morgan had waited
as the others fired. He did get off two shots, both
of them into the trees over the lean-tos. When the
call came to mount up, he was slower than the
others stepping into the saddle. He had been on a
cavalry charge once before when he had scouted for
the army and it had not been his favorite
experience.

As the second bugle call came, he hung back,
letting the regulars go over the top of the ridge and
ride down the other side. Some of them were firing

their rifles as they galloped forward. Damn good way to waste ammunition, he decided.

By the time the men were halfway across the 300 yard valley, he had barely made it down the slope. He moved across the dusty, parched land that had only occasional splotches of grass, and saw the fight ahead of him. A round or two slammed through the air past him but he had no idea if they were from friend or foe.

He heard gunfire to the north and figured a few of the red men had made it to their horses and tried to make a break for it. The river and its brush and cover would be their best and probably only hope.

The troopers stormed on horseback to the lean-tos, put away their rifles and used pistols, tearing down shelters with ropes around poles, rousting out Apaches where they huddled in the brush and cut them down as they ran for the stream.

It was all over in little less than seven minutes. Morgan came from the north where he had checked the Indian ponies. The detail of six men there said they had killed eight Chiricahua who sprinted for the horseflesh. Nobody had made it past them. To the south it had been much the same but there the troopers suffered four casualties. All were wounded, but not seriously. The Apaches had moved with more stealth and fired at the invaders first, driving them out of the brush and woods and then storming past before the troopers could recover and chase them.

At the main camp, they were mopping up a few places where a dozen or so Chiricahuas had taken refuge. They were in a small cave in the side of the hill near the creek and entirely out of sight in the brush.

Morgan watched as the troopers systematically shot down every Chiricahua in the shallow cave, and those who tried to break out. Only three of them had rifles.

Morgan turned away. He'd never seen a more calculated, brutal slaughter of human beings in his life. Not that he was a lily white proponent of non-violence.

Major Phelps rode up beaming. "Damn, but we're giving it to them dirty Apaches! I don't think more than eight or ten of them bastards got away! Going to make a beautiful report."

He turned to call to an officer.

"Lieutenant, see that every one of these shelters is torn down and burned. I don't want a stick left that they can use. Destroy any food you find, break up all pots and burn everything that will take a torch. Get it started."

The burning began. They found two wounded warriors in one of the lean-tos. Two quick shots solved the prisoner problem.

Morgan sat near the Blue River downstream from the last shelter. He could feel the heat of the fire. He threw stones in the creek. His buckskin stood munching some late fall grass in the shade of the trees.

This was the army way of solving problems. Practical, quick, effective, and better left alone without a good long look. He was certainly earning his two-dollars a day. He had about decided to ride his army mount into the first town of any size they came near and say goodbye to army life.

A horseman rode toward him and Morgan looked up at Major Phelps.

"There you are, Morgan. You found yourself a nice spot. Got a job for you. We're about wrapped up here. We'll go downstream a mile and rest up until my scout comes back from upstream. I want to make sure there's no more Chiricahaus up on the Blue. About decided that the stream is getting too small to support much of a camp.

"Anyway, we're stuck here for the rest of the morning, I'd guess. I want you and Gimpy to go find Captain Casemore over on the San Francisco River. As I remember from the map, it runs up there about 20 to 25 miles with a couple of branches and tributaries.

"Want you to go and find Casemore and see if he's turned up anything. If he hasn't, and he's more than ten miles up from the Blue, turn him around and bring him back to the junction with the Blue. By then we'll have this half of the unit waiting for you there."

Morgan remembered the map. "The San Francisco goes almost due east from where we left it before it turns north. Be quicker for us to go back down to the fork and up the San Francisco that way."

"Suit yourself. Try and find him before dark if you can, and come back down there tomorrow."

Morgan stood. "Where's Gimpy?"

The major pointed. The Apache stood less than four feet in back of Morgan who grinned. He signed, "Sneaky Buffalo Calf," and both scouts laughed.

Morgan mounted his buckskin and turned downstream. He stopped and looked back. "Oh, Major. How was your casualty count?"

"Six wounded, none seriously, no dead. Every man ready for duty."

"Congratulations," Morgan said, not meaning it as the major beamed and hurried away on some major type mission.

"Let's ride," Morgan signed to Gimpy.

"Before the sun dies," Gimpy signed in return.

Morgan remembered the Chiricahua warriors who had escaped down the Blue to the south. He swung to the far side of the valley and rode south as far from the cover along the stream as he could.

Gimpy nodded his agreement with the route and they picked up the pace to get to the San Francisco and start their chase of the other half of the task force.

They worked down the Blue quickly and covered the distance to the juncture of the two streams in less than two hours. The four supply wagons on the trip had been left there with the rest of the 350 men from Major Phelps' party, when the two units had headed out on their search and control missions.

Morgan was glad to see the wagons as they came out of some brush about 50 yards from them. Almost at once, a rifle shot slammed through the air near them and Morgan jerked his mount to the left. He slid out of the saddle and hit the ground ducking down behind the buckskin.

"What the hell you doing?" Morgan called.

"Jeez, I saw an Indian," a voice called back.

"He's our scout, asshole. We're coming in."

"We had some problems," the voice answered.

Morgan and Gimpy rode up to the four wagons. Three of them had been burned, ruined, with their loads. They all still smoked. The fourth wagon was singed but in good shape.

Stretched out under the wagon were two men, both with arrows in them, both dead.

"Damn," Morgan said. "Phelps is going to have a heart attack. When did this happen?"

"About two hours ago. Six of them came out of the brush and shot Johnny and Paul there before we knew they were here. Me and Grady got to cover and then they burned the wagons. I killed one of them, out there, but the five others carried him away."

"Where's Grady?"

"He's hiding in the woods. He kind of flipped out when we got attacked."

"Hold tough. Major Phelps will be back here before dark. He cut up about 80 to 85 Apaches upstream if that's any help. These were some of the few who got away."

"Goddamn!"

"We're going up the San Francisco to find Captain Casemore," Morgan told the man. "You remember to tell him we were here and left, all right?"

"Yeah, sure. I ain't caved in, it's Grady."

Morgan looked around. "Hey, where are the rest of the men? We left 350 troopers here."

"Oh, the lieutenant didn't like this for a camp site. He took them a mile back down the San Francisco."

Morgan snorted. "He better have a better excuse than that when the Major gets back. Looks like we lost most of our food for the next three weeks. My suggestion is that you ride like hell down to their camp, tell that lieutenant what happened and tell him he better send back 30 men with you to guard what's left of the rations and equipment or the major is going to bust him right down to a private in charge of shoveling the horseshit out of the stables. Go now."

The private stared at him, nodded, and took off on a run downstream. He didn't have a horse. He held his rifle in front of him at port arms.

Morgan and Gimpy looked at the rations that were left in the wagon, decided against them and rode across the Blue and started up the San Francisco.

The first ten miles went by quickly. The river kept on its easterly course through a series of gentle valleys that were barely big enough to be called that. The stream chattered as it dropped down and the riders kept climbing.

They had just worked their horses up to a steep

slope past a small falls and came through some trees into the start of a modest valley, when they saw sun flashes at the far end.

Morgan lifted his binoculars and checked the flashes. He saw a battle going on about a mile down the valley. There were enough blue shirts to convince him it was the other half of their task force. But who were they fighting?

"Big Trouble," Morgan signed and both men kicked their mounts into a gallop and rode hard through the short grass of the valley toward the not-so-distant battle.

Chapter Six

The fighting was over by the time Morgan and Gimpy rode up to the army troops. They were infantry, evidently the tail end of the Casemore column. From the looks of things, the troops had been hit from the rear and both sides by a considerable force of hostiles.

Morgan tried to find some officer in charge but there seemed to be only a sergeant. He was wounded with a rifle bullet through his chest and sat under a tree. A private tried to stop the bleeding.

"Don't know where the hell they came from," the sergeant said in a small, soft voice. "One minute we was hiking up this damn stream and the next we had them savages all over us. They got us in a cross fire and then charged us on foot."

He coughed and spit up a gout of blood. The sergeant shivered. "Damn, but it's getting cold out. Anyway, them damn savages charged us on foot with rifles and knives. They cut off about 50 of us and just sliced us to pieces. Most of my men have single shot rifles and they never got off more than one shot."

A half dozen calvary troopers rode up in a swirl of dust. A lieutenant jumped down and hurried to the sergeant.

"Murdock, what the hell happened here?"

"We had a tea party, Lieutenant. What the hell does it look like?"

The young officer's face got red and he looked around at Morgan and Gimpy.

"Soldier, you can't talk to me that way. I asked you a question?"

"Lieutenant, shut your mouth," Morgan said, pushing him aside. "The man is dying, can't you see that?"

The officer stared at Morgan for a minute, then stood and stepped into his saddle and began to take charge. He got the wounded together under some trees. The field surgeon who had been sent with his column soon arrived from the front of the march and began patching up the bleeding bodies.

The sergeant looked at Morgan and grinned. "Thanks, scout. I appreciate that. Damned officers. It was about 50 Apaches, all of them had rifles and bows and arrows and knives. Damn, them bastards are fighting machines. They won, we lost."

The sergeant looked over at Morgan. He gave a small sigh and died, his eyes staring sightlessly at the afternoon sun.

It was another ten minutes before Captain Casemore got back to the end of the column. He rode around on his horse, put out a circle of cavalry as guards, and checked the men.

Morgan rode up to him and delivered the message from Major Phelps.

Casemore was short and chunky, fat cheeks

slightly red and thinning blonde hair. He swore, "Christ, I was getting ready to send a hundred cavalry after that bunch of hostiles. I've got my scouts out finding their trail. They're bound to go downstream."

He glared at Morgan for a minute. "Take me an hour to get this column back on the road. I'm sending out my cavalry to run down those damn savages. A field situation decision." He nodded to convince himself, then rode off.

Morgan went back to the wounded men. He found one who had an arrow in his shoulder waiting for the doctor.

"Trooper, how many of them were there, any idea?"

"Maybe 50. They were on us before we knew what happened. They cut us off from the unit right ahead. Damn, they were good. I've never seen an Indian fight before."

"Moved like lightning, they did," a man beside him said. He had a rifle round through his thigh. "We killed maybe four or five, but they dragged them off into the brush and were gone."

"You see any women or kids?"

"Hell, no! These was fighting men, and how they fought!"

"Apache?"

"Hell, how would we know?"

Morgan chuckled. "Yeah, I understand. You guys take it easy now, the doctor is coming."

It was two hours before the troops were on the march again. They had no wagons. The dead were put on travois pulled by cavalry ponies. Nine men had died. Four others were wounded so severely that they couldn't ride and were put on travois as well. The travois were made with long poles braced apart by a cross arm to form a triangle, then wrapped with army blankets. It was slow going.

One of the wounded men died a mile downstream.

The captain had sent a hundred of his cavalry out on the trail of the hostiles. A messenger came back reporting they had picked up the trail of the Apaches heading downstream, probably at a trot. The horses were keeping up with them but not able to close the gap.

The scouts estimated that the Apaches were about three miles ahead of them.

Captain Casemore had put half of his remaining cavalry at the lead and half at the end of his column. They were not going to make it back to the junction with the Blue River before darkness.

Morgan checked out with the captain, then he and Gimpy rode fast to get back to the rest of the forces. He kept watching for the cavalry unit tracking the hostiles, but they were all the way to the Blue River before he realized they hadn't seen the cavalry. Strange. That meant that the Apaches had cut across some ridges they figured the horses couldn't climb.

Morgan and Gimpy arrived at the camp below the Blue just as dusk settled over the campsite. The three wagons had been gutted of any useful gear and supplies, then the rest of the wreckage burned. The smell of cooking and burning salt pork saturated the whole camp area for a while.

Morgan found the major and gave him a report.

"So if the hostiles came this way, they must have by-passed us by now or turned off into the hills. Damn, wish you could go out in the dark and try to cut a trail. You and Gimpy check them out first thing tomorrow. If we can find a trail going past us, we'll put out a fresh troop of cavalry tracking the bastards."

The major looked up from his late supper. "How

many men did Casemore lose?"

"Ten, last count. Three men seriously wounded."

"You know this country, Morgan?"

"Pretty well."

"How far are we from a food supply?"

"Used to be a little crossroads community called Clifton down the San Francisco River maybe 12, 15 miles from here. There used to be about 40 people living there. They wouldn't have enough food for breakfast for a thousand men."

"Where else?"

"Next spot would be Fort Thomas on the Gila. The San Francisco runs into the Gila so we're going downstream." Morgan looked to the west. They were on a good enough rise to see some distance.

"See that peak over there, sir? That should be Bryce Mountain. We can go cross country and hang just to the north of that peak and we should hit Fort Thomas on the nose. From here, we'll have about 50 miles."

"Two days on quarter rations. We should be able to do that. Since we had the wagons, the men didn't carry their usual four to five days of salt pork and hardtack."

The major took a long look west, then nodded. "All right. I'm still going to follow those hostiles. I'll keep 150 cavalry troopers and most of the rations left. We'll keep the Indian scouts and try to live off the land. I want those hostiles. How many did they say there were?"

"About 50, Major."

"Good. I'll send the wagon back and we'll back 10 to 12 days food on our horses. Ten pounds of grain per horse should be on the mounts; quarter rations for two days for the rest of the troops. You have your choice, Morgan. Go with me and stay employed, or return to Fort Thomas and be out of work. I want you with me."

The major and the supply sergeant spent an hour working over the available rations. At last they had it worked out. The cavalry had left with eight days rations in their saddlebags. This was the fourth day. The returning cavalry would give up two days rations to the sergeant.

The 150 troopers to continue the campaign would be given four more days rations. That would be 16 days worth of food on half day rations. They would take along one of the wagon horses and butcher it the second day.

The troops to march to Fort Thomas would use the remaining rations. They would come out to nearly half rations per day per man.

"More than adequate," Major Phelps said. He had his orderly find Morgan and bring him to the Sibley tent. It would be going back with the wagon.

"Have you decided about going on the hunt for the hostiles?"

"I'll go with you, Major. Is Gimpy coming?"

"Yes, the six Indian scouts will be with us. The four civilian scouts will lead the column back to Fort Thomas."

Morgan went back to a small campfire where he and Gimpy were signing. The Apache was 27 years old, had two wives back at the fort, and would ride with the army until they no longer would hire him. He had grown up in New Mexico and across the border into Mexico as well.

"Where would the force head that hit Casemore's column?" Morgan asked him by sign.

Gimpy stared into the fire then pointed deeper into the San Francisco Mountains, then waved to the south.

"The Chiricahuas in this area love a certain range of mountains to the south. But they would head into the mountains here and then work south. They will try to get to the Peloncillos. Rugged, high, steep." He signed all this and it took some time, but Morgan was patient.

"I have heard of this range," Morgan signed.

"We chase them?" Gimpy asked.

"Tomorrow we leave."

"It is not good to sit still in the mountains. The mountain spirits like their children to play and move about."

"We'll really make them happy tomorrow," Morgan said.

He made the sign for sleep and spread out his blanket. He would try to get an extra one before the wagon left tomorrow. The mountains were cold at night now that it was September.

The next morning, Captain Casemore and his column marched into the camp. Casemore had a long conference with the major inside the Sibley tent and voices were raised.

At once, the food distribution took place. Major Phelps took one of the troops that had seen action with him, and selected two more. The troops normally would have 100 men in each, but with the lowered troop strength, most units were lucky to have 50 to 55 members.

Casemore did not seem happy about being sent with the column to Fort Thomas. His command had been bloodied and he wanted to be in on the kill. But he followed his orders.

By noon, the 150 cavalry troops were supplied, drew extra ammuntion and were ready to go.

Morgan had forgotten about the cavalry Captain Casemore had sent out to track the hostiles. He asked the Major.

"Oh, they tracked the Apaches when they left the river and turned up into the San Francisco

Mountains. After two miles, the lieutenant in charge turned his men around and went back to the column."

"Be helpful if they could show us where the savages turned into the hills," Morgan said. "Be damn helpful, if we're gonna find them. There's just one hell of a lot of ground out here if we start checking every square foot for moccasin prints."

"Morgan, your irony is not appreciated. If you weren't a good tracker and scout, I'd fire you in a second. I'll have two of the troopers on that ride detailed to come with us and point out where the trail left the river. Then they can return to their unit."

Major Lewiston Phelps led the troopers back up the San Francisco River just after one P.M. They had 158 troopers, officers and scouts. Two of the men had been slightly wounded on the Blue River fight, but they asked to be allowed to accompany their troop. Permission was granted.

Two hours later, they came to the spot along the river where the hostiles had crossed and headed north toward the higher peaks. The two troopers from the other company were released and headed back toward the rest of the column below the Blue.

There was no trouble tracking them for the first two miles. There were what looked like 1,000 army hoof prints blocking out the signs that had been left by the Chiricahuas. Then the army prints stopped and Gimpy and Morgan moved to the front and got off their mounts, walking along a trail that was now only a hint and a promise. By now the trail was over 24 hours old.

They moved generally north for a mile, then scaled a ridge that was sharp but not too much for the horses. At that point there was evidence that the hostiles had rested just over the ridge evidently watching their back trail. They found the remains of a rabbit that had been taken probably by arrow to prevent the noise of a gunshot.

Gimpy circled the area twice, then came back grinning. "Turn south," he signed. There was a "told you so" expression on the weathered Apache face. Now the signs were more evident. The Apaches probably had waited for the pursuit, saw the cavalry unit turn back and now felt safe enough to travel faster with less effort at concealment of their trail.

They had just entered a small valley with a tiny trickle of water in the bottom, and were moving across it, when Gimpy went into the lead and Morgan came behind him. They changed the lead often to rest their eyes and attention.

Gimpy found the trail leading directly across the small creek and he stepped toward a smattering of brush. Suddenly he jumped back, and cried out in alarm.

Morgan dropped to one knee, his Spencer up and ready. He saw nothing but the dagger-edged, foot-long piece of cactus fly by a foot over his head.

Gimpy was down. Morgan ran forward ten-feet and found the scout on his back, slowly picking a two foot long cactus branch from his bare chest. The thorns were half an inch long and gently curved. When they stabbed into flesh they were difficult to get out.

Morgan touched Gimpy's hand and stopped him. Morgan looked at the thorns, saw the direction of the penetration, and using his knife point, began to ease one barb after another out of the weathered skin and sturdy flesh.

Gimpy had been bare to the waist since the trip started. It had provided his reddish brown skin with a golden glow. Now that glow as spattered with blood. The first thorns to come out were the most shallow in penetration. Morgan used his riding gloves and a stick to hold the cactus off the flesh once it was free.

Major Phelps rode up and dismounted.

"What seems to be the holdup here?" he crackled as he walked up to his scouts on the ground. He looked over Morgan's shoulder and grunted.

"By God, they got him," Phelps said.

"Be another five minutes, Major. I'd be cautious about entering the brush until we check it out."

Morgan edged the last thorn out of flesh and threw the stickery object into the brush.

He used a neckerchief to stop the flow of blood. Then he wet the kerchief from his canteen and wiped the blood off Gimpy's chest. The small Apache grinned all the time, even though Morgan knew it was hurting like a dozen spots of fire on his chest. He sat up and Morgan insisted that he take a drink.

The Apache held up his hands and signed. "Don't-follow-me-trap," he said. "Chiricahua famous for them."

Morgan trampled the grass and light brush for 20 feet on both sides of the trap. It had been a simple snare with the two pieces of deadly cactus stems held in readiness by a bent back sapling. When the snare trigger was released by a footstep, the snare activated, releasing the thin cord that held the sapling down.

The troop went across the creek, paused to refill their canteens, then let their horses drink.

Morgan put Gimpy in his saddle. "There'll be more signs now. The Chiricahua won't think anyone will follow them now," Morgan signed to the small man. Gimpy had put on an army blue shirt. It was the smallest issued but still much too big for him.

Gimpy sat sullen for a momemt. "Caught me in damn trap," he signed. "Gimpy damn mad!"

Morgan watched and laughed. He signed back. "I'm damn glad that you're alive . . . and mad."

Chapter Seven

Morgan tracked the hostiles the rest of the day. They were moving fast, he could tell by the spurts of sand dug up by the toes as the moccasins came off the ground. A trot, a six-miles an hour trot. The Apaches could be 25 miles ahead of them by now. Any sudden rain or bad winstorm would wipe out the tracks for good.

As Morgan thought of it, he saw thunderheads building up in front of them to the south. Great snowy balls of clouds were punched up from rising heat on the ground. They spiraled thousands of feet in the air looking like great rounded mounds of whipped cream that his mother used to make.

The column was headed right at them. Morgan rode over to the major and mentioned the clouds, but the officer merely nodded and went back to chewing a wad of tobacco in his right jaw.

"If it comes, it comes. Not a damn thing we can do about it."

"True enough, but I want you to know that nobody can track a trail this old after a cloudburst." Morgan had the last word and rode ahead to where Gimpy had started to get off his horse.

"No," Morgan bellowed from behind the scout. He straightened and waited.

"My turn," Gimpy signed.

"Say it in English. From now on we talk English, no signing. You know more English than I know your tongue."

"My turn," Gimpy said in slightly accented English.

"Good talking, but it's still my turn. You see any plants or herbs along here you want to put on those thorn slashes on your chest?"

Gimpy looked up at Morgan not able to follow it.

"Medicine herbs, chest," Morgan said.

"Ah, find one." Gimpy said haltingly. "One more."

Morgan nodded and went back to the trail. It had turned due south now and a mile on they picked up a creek and moved downstream.

"Gila," Gimpy said. "Behind the mountains, Peloncillo."

Morgan rode back to the major and told him the development. "Gimpy says the Chiricahuas like these next mountains, the Peloncillo. They have a lot of favorite spots and some camps built in there from what he told me. The Gila River runs behind them, so we can go around this end, or over them, or around the other end."

"Let's see what the hostiles do before we decide," Major Phelps said.

The trail was still distinct only because the Chiricahua thought they had lost their trackers. With any effort at all they could have concealed a trail well enough that after this long it would be worthless, not even another Apache could follow it.

The major called a halt at about four that afternoon. They were still drifting downstream on the Gila, so there would be plenty of water for the horses and the men. A little grass would give the mares some forage.

Once the column stopped, the complicated routine of a cavalry camp began. The animals came first. The troopers put up picket lines for the horses and then they were fed and watered.

The men now moved to assigned tasks. Each of the three companies settled into areas of its own and they posted guards around each company's perimeter. Details usually sent to find water had it the easiest, and the fuel detail for each company found all the fuel it needed in the brush along the high water mark where sticks and branches and a few logs were stuck in the growth.

The men set up their two man pup tents, this time in random groups.

Next came the most welcome routine of the day, the evening chow call. Food on the trail was the responsibility of each man. On this march it was salt pork and hardtack. Salt pork was famous for being the worst food in the army, and that most often served on marches and campaigns.

It was usually half spoiled when given out. After another five days in the boiling sun it was riper yet. It had to be parboiled and then fried, and sometimes mixed with a little water. The hardtack was like a slab of rock and became edible only when it was crumpled and soaked in water. By mashing it and mixing it with the salt pork, the men had a fairly palatable meal.

It was sometimes more work to get the salt pork ready to eat than it was worthwhile to gulp it down. But on most marches that's all there was.

Morgan struggled with his, until Gimpy took

charge. He had one of the big tin cups he used over the fire and boiled the salt pork, then mixed the hardtack in. When that was ready, he pulled a small cotton tail rabbit from his pack and skinned it.

"When shoot that?" Morgan asked him.

"While you wiped down your horse," Gimpy signed.

Morgan laughed and had another good meal. The best part was the boiled coffee and the roast rabbit.

Sleep was the next order of the day. Some of the troops used the small amount of daylight left to play cards, write letters and gossip with friends. Morgan spent the time digging a hole for his hips in the soft ground beneath the trees and scraping up a bed out of the leaf mold that carpeted the ground under the trees.

Morgan then looked at Gimpy's chest. The thorn marks were turning red. Gimpy nodded and asked for his cup. Morgan brought it half filled with water. Gimpy set it on the coals to heat, and took out a length of green herb that he had picked somewhere and a root that looked like a long green onion. He mashed the two together, then poured out most of the water from the cup, put the pulp into it and boiled it for three or four minutes. When most of the water had boiled away, he worked the soft pulp with a stick until it was a greenish putty, then while it was still hot he dabbed the poultice on the red, ugly wounds on his chest from the cactus thorns. He let it dry, then lay on his back and motioned and Morgan spread the rest of the greenish mixture on the cuts and punctures until they all were covered.

"Sleep," Gimpy said and he closed his eyes and almost at once was sleeping.

Yeah, sleep, Morgan thought and settled into his own fixed up bed. It was surprisingly soft. Better than he'd had since he left the bunk at the fort. He slept.

When Morgan awoke in the morning, he looked over to where Gimpy had been and saw that the Apache was gone. He wondered if the scout had experienced a change of heart and decided to go warn the hostiles.

No, his horse was where he had left it. Morgan looked the other way and found Gimpy at the stream washing the poultice off his chest. He came back and warmed himself by the small fire he had already built. Morgan looked at his chest. The redness was gone, the puffiness around the worst slashes was down.

Gimpy went about the process of making a new poultice. He knew there would not be a chance for another fire until late that afternoon. He got the poultice mashed and boiled and applied it all himself this time.

Morgan watched the camp come alive. He didn't know all of the cavalry routine, but he remembered most of it.

First Call came at 4:45 A.M. The men rolled out of their blankets.

Reveille and Stable Call at 4:55. They had ten minutes to get their horses saddled and ready to ride.

Mess Call at 5:00. Now they had 30 minutes to fix whatever breakfast they could. Usually it was without a fire. This was one of the most relaxed periods of their morning.

General call at 5:30. They struck their tents, stowed everything on board their mounts and got ready to ride.

Boots and Saddles at 5:45. Every man mounted and in formation ready to move out.

Forward March, at 6:00. The column was formed

up and ready to move out at six in the morning.

It was too early a start for Morgan. He never could tolerate army life. As a scout, he did not have to follow the routine. But he did have to be ready to ride at six. Oftentimes he had been out in front scouting the trail by this time. This morning he watched Gimpy fix his thorn stings.

Then they were riding. Major Phelps said they would keep following the trail wherever it led.

"We were lucky yesterday avoiding the rain. I just hope that it didn't rain across the trail ahead sometime yesterday."

Five miles up the Gila River, the hostiles turned sharply to the west and trotted toward the mountains. Twice now they had found where the band of Indians had stopped for a time to eat. There had been feathers at one place, and two rabbit skins at another. The skins had been stretched on sticks and Gimpy had tied them on his horse. He said the hunter had intended taking the skins with him, but forgot them.

Morgan checked with the major. "The hostiles are moving out to those mountains we talked about, going around this end or over some of the low ones on this end. We stay on their tracks?"

"Yes." The major looked up at the thunderheads which had appeared out of nowhere in an hour. "What's the chances of rain?"

The light breeze blew toward them, out of the west. The sky darkened below the thunderheads and they just *looked* wet.

"Major, I'd say about nine chances out of ten that we get wet this afternoon or tonight."

"Morgan, I want you to fix it so we catch the bastards before then."

"That might take some doing, Major. Once they get into these mountains it's like a stronghold. Not sure we have enough fire power to drive them out."

"We'll see about that," Major Phelps said and turned back to the head of the column.

By midday they had traveled over some low hills and the hostiles turned south again on the far side of the Peloncillo mountains.

Before they started down the broad valley in front of the mountains, Gimpy signed to Morgan. A moment later Morgan asked the major to stop the column for a conference. The soldier frowned, then nodded and called the halt.

"Major Phelps, Gimpy and I think it would be better scouting to keep the troops here and let us head on down the trail and try to locate the hostiles. If we let them know now that we are here in force, they will have plenty of time to fort up, or to vanish into caves and canyons of these mountains and we might never find them."

"Gimpy told you all that?"

"In a lot fewer words. I think he's right. We could camp here and Gimpy and I could make a try at finding where they have holed up."

"What makes you think they haven't kept going straight to Mexico?"

"If they wanted to be in Mexico, why the swing to this side of the mountains? It's closer by staying on the other side."

"I'll be damned! You always seem to have the right answers. Well, we've done well so far, and this time I tend to agree with you. How far is the nearest river over this side of the mountains?"

"That would be the San Simon out about ten more miles due west."

"Too far, we'll find an arroyo and dry camp. You want to go in there at night, I'd guess."

"Damn right. I don't cotton to the idea of getting my brains boiled out over some Apache fire."

"Thought the Comanches did that?"

"A lot of the tribes use that form of torture."

The line of march had stopped and now Morgan looked for a camping spot. He found it in a small ravine about a mile farther on. It was dry, but they were mostly out of sight of the tallest peak on this end of the range. He just hoped that there was no Chiricahuas on lookout up there, watching their back trail.

There was no shade. The sun beat down and the men set up their tents just to find shade, leaving both ends open for the wind to blow through. Only there wasn't any wind.

The 158 men sweated and waited.

Morgan and Gimpy talked about the scouting. It was mostly in sign now so there would be no mistakes.

They knew they had to trail the band into the mountains, but how did they find the correct valley or gully to go up if they couldn't track them during the day?

At last they decided they would ride in, hide their horses, and then check the possible entrances by daylight. Which meant it might take them two or three days to find the right entrance that the Apaches used.

Morgan talked to the major about it.

"Three days just to figure out which gully they took? Damn, no! We don't have that much time."

"We've got 16 days, Major Phelps. We've used two of them. It's a better gamble to spend two or three more now and get a reading on them, then charge in there, let them react to us and then we try to run them down. Most places back in there a horse can't move. I've heard that's why the Apaches like it so well. I don't want to get into a contest with the Apaches with me on foot."

"Hell. This hasn't been the best patrol I've ever led. Damn, go ahead. Three days, then we're moving in and stir them up and pick a fight, whether you're back or not. If we find you strung up over some cooking fire, we'll cut you down. Agreed?"

Morgan scowled at the major and went back to tell Gimpy the news. First, he checked the Apache's chest. The green muddy poultice was still on his skin, only now it had faded out to a muddy gray.

"One more day," Gimpy signed.

They talked about the horses. "Might be better to leave them here," Morgan said.

Gimpy looked at him. "You do Indian trot?"

"A couple of hours at a time I can do, but that don't mean I can go ten hours."

Gimpy nodded. He touched Morgan's uniform pants and shirt. "You have brown clothes?"

Morgan dug into his blanket roll and took out a brown pair of pants and a sun-tan shirt.

"Wear them," Gimpy signed.

"We won't need to wait until dark if we go on foot," Morgan signed. Gimpy nodded.

They took their revolvers, no rifles, a pack of food on their backs and two canteens of water each.

"You're crazy," Major Phelps said watching them get ready. He'd heard that the scouts were going in without horses and he came to check.

"Crazy and alive is better than stark raving sane and hanging upside down over that cooking fire." Morgan laughed softly at the major's reaction. He and Gimpy each drank half a canteen of water, filled theirs up again, and started for the mountains at a slow trot.

Chapter Eight

Morgan and Gimpy had found a slight rise near the cavalry's temporary location and checked out the country between them and the foothills of the Peloncillo Mountains. They worked out a route that would allow them to move almost to the edge of the hills while remaining in a series of small ravines.

The shallow arroyos were everywhere, indicating to Morgan that the country had more than its share of cloudbursts, or at least heavy rains all at once, and the water couldn't all be absorbed into the soil so it had to run off to lower ground.

The runoff gouged out the gullies and after each rain they became deeper.

The pair of runners worked along the main ravine where the rest of the unit hid. By that time they were well out of sight of their troops.

Gimpy put up a hand and stopped. "Not used to running this way. Army horses have spoiled me." He signed it.

Morgan laughed and signed "Me too," and they both panted to get back their breath.

They moved ahead slower then, trotting here and there, walking, always watching the slopes ahead of them for any sign of life. Once Morgan thought he saw a gun glint from high on the nearest peak, but after watching it for several minutes, he decided it was only a flash of the sun off some stationary swatch of mica or some other glistening rock.

After an hour, they had come to within a few hundred yards of the mountains. There were few foothills. Most of the peaks rose up from the desert and seemed higher than they really were. The two scouts angled for the first good sized opening into the mountains, a wide dry wash that seemed to come directly from the barren uplifts, but when they came closer they saw there was a small slice of a valley between two thrusting peaks.

Morgan remembered from the map that there was only one sizeable mountain in the string, and that just a little over 6,000 feet.

They came toward the main wash with caution. There was no way they could approach or inspect the wash for signs of footprints or moccasin impressions without being seen.

"We wait for darkness?" Morgan asked as they sat in the shade of a small overhang in a gully 50 yards from the side of the wash.

"No see them," Gimpy signed.

He put a headband on, pulled a pair of moccasins from his pants pocket and slipped them on. He wore no shirt. He unbuckled his gunbelt and handed it to Morgan.

"One Indian look for prints in wash," he signed.

Morgan started to protest, but he knew it was the only way. If someone saw Gimpy, he would think it was another Chiricahua coming in or hunting or on a scouting trip.

Gimpy moved out at a six mile trot. It was a good thing he had a short distance. He came to the first part of the wash and began sweeping the area with his glance as he swung his head back and forth.

Gimpy worked across the mouth of the wash where it led into the mountains, then he did the same thing on his trip back. He dropped into the gully and took a small drink from the canteen on his gunbelt.

"No Indians go up trail," he signed.

They worked down two more small ravines to the next opening into the mountains. It was past two smaller hills and they had a chance to get closer to the mouth of the little valley that led inward.

Gimpy shed his army gear and made his search. This time he stayed on the far side and signaled for Morgan to come across. He did, moving at a slow and steady pace, trying not to catch the attention of any far off lookout. When he slid in beside a shadowed rock, he looked at Gimpy.

The Apache's eyes sparkled. "Many feet pass here," he said in English.

"Any travois?" Morgan asked.

"Ten, maybe twelve."

"Which means a permanent camp, women and children along."

Gimpy held up a small carved figure about four inches long. "Child toy," Gimpy signed.

"We have to go up the valley and find their camp," Morgan signed. The Apache's eyes glinted again. Morgan frowned forming worry lines on his forehead.

"Gimpy, did the Chiricahuas hurt your band at some time?" Morgan signed.

The Apache laughed but anger showed through. "Chiricahua attack my band, kill my wife and child, give me bad leg, run off all of our horses. All but four our men were hunting. Never trust a Chiricahua."

Morgan nodded. "Thanks," he said, then pointed up the small valley. "After dark," he said in English and signed. The Apache understood and they both sat down to wait for the end of the day. Already the sun had slid behind the far western ridges.

Morgan wanted to ask the sinew thin, hard as desert rocks Apache how long ago it had been since the Chiricahuas attacked his band, but he didn't think this was the time. He was sure he knew more about the small man than anyone else at the fort. It was enough. Gimpy hated the Chiricahua. He would track them down for the almost equally hated Pony Soldiers.

As they waited in the concealing darkness, they nibbled on the hardtack. Gimpy dripped water on his rock hard pieces of heavy cracker until it was soft enough to eat. Morgan did the same. It tasted like cardboard but would put something in his stomach besides water. There was no native food nearby. Perhaps in the ravine in the mountains.

As dusk descended over the valley, they watched a pair of night hawks slant out into the open country looking for a good meal. They swooped low, scouring the dry land for some game. A short time later a night hawk screamed in the darkness.

Gimpy looked up, his head cocked one way listening. After several seconds passed and there was no reply to the call, he nodded. "Bird, not Chiricahua," he said in English.

As soon as it was fully dark, they stood and walked forward up the same path that dozens of moccasined feet and at least ten travois had used. The trail would be direct now, no need for hiding it.

The two scouts could make out the drag marks

of the heavily laden travois in the soft moonlight, but they were not now looking for tracks, but for the people who made them. Somewhere up in this forbidding wilderness of crags and peaks and dry gullies and stark mountains, there was a large band of Indians, probably Chiricahua.

The small valley led forward, narrowed suddenly and then widened for another quarter mile. Suddenly it ended. Only a narrow ravine led forward. They could see where the travois had passed this way. Gimpy stood and pointed forward.

They checked in an arc around the end of the travois tracks, but could find nothing. The faint moonlight was enough to see where the travois tracks had made a deep impression in the sand and dirt, then suddenly the marks were gone.

"Brushed out," Morgan said to Gimpy. "Why would they do that? And where the hell did they all go?"

Gimpy and Morgan began to check the seemingly solid rock walls ahead and on both sides of them. There was a light growth of greasewood here and some other chaparral. Some of it grew 10 to 12 feet high. There was more rain here and the moisture must hit the rock wall and run down watering the brush.

They were halfway around, pushing aside the brush and small trees, examining the rock wall, when Morgan gave a shout. One section of the rock wall suddenly was not there. Instead, there was a black hole, a gap in the rocks.

Gimpy rushed up and looked. They both pushed back the brush on each side and found it wide enough for a travois.

"Damn, we found it!" Morgan said. Gimpy nodded and walked forward. The opening was dark inside, but when they looked upward they could see a slice of sky. There were rocky walls on each side with little more than ten feet of space between. Upward, only a few stars could be seen in the blackness of space.

The hidden slice through the mountain had been made not by a watercourse that might flow through it after a heavy rain, but seemed to have been created when the mountain was torn apart by some massive earthquake or a violent eruption that blasted lava from a volcano as the world was being formed.

The path led gradually upward. Once they came to a place where an abrupt two foot step up must have given the horses pulling the travois fits. The frame must have been lifted up by a dozen sturdy Chiricahua warriors.

After what seemed to be a half mile, but must have only been 200 or 300 yards, the split mountain ended and they came out into a changed world.

The very air was softer, more humid, and cooler. Somehow there was a sense of Idaho here that Morgan couldn't understand. He touched Gimpy's shoulder and the smaller man frowned.

"A garden, flowers, water," he signed.

Morgan nodded. "Yes, water." He looked up and saw the dark shapes of the mountain towering above them. It was a small valley with the sharp steep slabs of basalt and granite jolting skyward like the tall buildings did in St. Louis. Morgan wondered if the valley here was more than 100 yards wide.

Why was there no lookout, no Indian scout watching their back trail? He and Gimpy had squatted as soon as they felt the change in the air. Now they stood, backs against the rocks and stared ahead.

It was mostly black, but far ahead, they could see

the glow of a fire, or perhaps more than one.

"Must look," Gimpy said softly and they stepped forward, cautiously, making sure they made not the slightest sound. If they were discovered they would die, and die so slowly they would be screaming for release in death long before it happened.

What Morgan took to be a valley, they soon discovered to be little more than a wide canyon. They found a small stream that evidently vanished underground almost at the base of the rocky wall. The two walked cautiously along beside it so its low chatter would cover any noise of their movement.

If there were no guards outside, surely there would be none in here. The hidden entrance made this an ideal stronghold. Two good men with rifles could hold off a thousand men out there.

They had moved cautiously 50 yards along the small stream when they came to what looked like a garden. There were rows of plants, ditches to irrigate them. Morgan bent down and felt the soil. It was heavy, he guessed black, ideal soil for growing plants, not like the sandy, rocky soil outside.

Gimpy spat in disgust. "Apache are not diggers in the dirt!" he whispered.

"Perhaps there are some Mandans here," Morgan said. "They were great farmers in North Dakota."

Now ahead they could see the fire plainly. It seemed to be a council fire of some type. Two dozen or more figures sat around the fire, some talking. Now they saw the shadows of wickiups around the fire. More were strung out along the small stream. One came into view in the darkness less than 30 feet ahead of them. Their movement that way was blocked.

Between the rocky wall and the wickiup there was scarcely 20 feet. Now Morgan guessed that the whole valley was less then 200 yards long, and perhaps only 50 yards wide. They swung away from the stream and the shelters and walked soundlessly to the far wall across green, springy grass. Trees and shrubs grew near the wall and for a moment they rested in the concealment.

"You see any women or children?" Morgan asked Gimpy.

They moved forward again then stopped and froze themselves against some of the small trees.

Two women left a wickiup crossed the river just below the council fire and walked to the woods where they squatted less than 20 feet from Morgan and relieved themselves. They chattered as they came and went. When they were back in their shelters, Morgan touched Gimpy.

"What were they talking about?" Morgan whispered.

"Woman talk, of babies, and cooking and finding roots and nuts and wishing they were in the forest of oak trees where they camped early last summer."

"So there are women and children," Morgan said. "Let's count the wickiups and get our asses out of here before they find us."

Gimpy shook his head. "Need to know what they council about. Perhaps to leave here soon."

He whispered the words in effective English, and Morgan realized the little Apache knew more English than he would usually admit.

They edged forward through the trees until they could belly up almost to the edge of the firelight. Gimpy listened to one after another of the warriors stand and speak. Each man could have his say, and most said a lot.

Gimpy started to work back away from the council fire. He had heard enough. Just then two young boys bounded out of a wickiup nearest the council fire and the boys ran directly for Gimpy where he lay in the woods.

They screeched with laughter as they turned away from the fire and urinated. Then one touched the other and the game of tag was on. One backed up and stepped on Gimpy. The boy lost his balance and fell directly on the Apache scout.

"Aiiiiiiieeeeeeee!" the Indian boy screeched at the top of his voice. He shouted another sentence and then screeched again. Gimpy jumped up and ran into the darkness away from the fire.

In a few seconds every warrior in the council had leaped to his feet, grabbed a torch and raced in the direction that Gimpy had run.

Morgan faded back from the fire as noiselessly as he could. He had been 10 feet behind Gimpy because he couldn't tell what the Indian words around the council fire meant. Now he was out of the path of the boys and the charging warriors.

Soon he came to the solid rock wall. He looked up. It was not perpendicular, but he would never be able to climb it and out of the gorge before daylight. He was trapped.

Morgan burrowed down in a patch of heavy brush and began creating a thicker screen for himself by pulling out dry weeds and grasses and weaving them in front of him. One of the searchers started Morgan's way with a brightly burning torch. He came within 20 feet, then a screech of victory echoed from down the canyon and the warrior turned and ran that way.

A short time later Morgan saw the warriors returning to the council fire. This time they had Gimpy. He had discarded everything that even hinted at the U.S. Army, including the cut off civilian pants he wore. He had a breechcloth on and no weapons as the Chiricahuas prodded him forward with the burned out torches until he stood before the council fire.

Two men stood with rifles aimed at Gimpy and the rest settled back down around the fire.

Morgan's first thought was to leave at once, while they were interested in Gimpy. But were they all there? Had they now posted guards at the start of the long tunnel like gorge to the outside? He had no way of knowing. Someone surely would find him by daylight.

Or would Gimpy convince them he was friendly, another Chiricahua lost during the raid. Not a chance. He was a Coyotero and these men would know the difference.

Morgan watched the council. As near as he could figure it out, this was some kind of a trial. Gimpy was bound now, his hands behind his back, and his feet tied together so he could stand and face them.

One tall Chiricahua with a lone eagle feather in his braid, repeatedly asked Gimpy questions. His answers were short and brought derisive laughter from the council.

Morgan had no idea what story Gimpy told. Whatever it was, the Chiricahua did not believe him. Soon it was obvious that he would be killed, the question seemed to be how it should be done.

Some of the warriors held up rifles, some bows and arrows, and a few ten foot long lances with feathers on them, and with bright steel points.

The man with the one eagle feather stood and lifted his hands. The talking stopped. He looked at each of the weapons and shook his head. The proponents sat down. He said a few words and the men jumped to their feet cheering.

Then the council broke up. Gimpy was led to a ten foot pole planted deeply in the ground at the edge of the council fire area. It was close enough to be seen in the light of the fire. The warriors tied Gimpy to the pole, with his hands high over his head. His back was against the pole and his feet pushed halfway around the pole and tied together so he couldn't really stand up. When he sagged it put pressure on his hands so he nearly hung by them.

Trying to stand and then using his arms would soon exhaust Gimpy completely.

This time a guard was left to watch Gimpy. Morgan didn't know if it was to see that he didn't die before morning, or to see that he didn't get away. The guard held a Spencer repeating rifle in his hands as if he knew how to use it.

Morgan stared at the sight. To leave or not to leave? If they caught him trying to escape, he would be in just as much trouble as Gimpy.

Slowly a plan began to form in his mind. The Chiricahua of all the Indians loved to see a brave man, an outrageously brave act of a fool or a hero, they saw no difference. It just might work. Yes it could, and at the same time it could keep the Chiricahua from being slaughtered by the cavalry. He'd witnessed one mass execution this week, that was enough.

Morgan settled down for the night. He wouldn't try to escape. He would work out his master scene and play it for all is life was worth. At this point he figured there was damn little else that he could do.

Chapter Nine

Twice during the long night Morgan woke up to hear Gimpy moaning. The way he was tied, half standing, half hanging was putting a strain on his muscles. With his hands fastened so high it prevented his lungs from working fully. The fire still burned nearby and the alert guard moved around watching things. There was nothing Morgan could do.

With dawn Morgan was ready.

He settled his six gun in leather, then took off his gunbelt and holding it in front of him he walked boldly through the fringes of the just waking camp to the biggest and best made wickiup.

These were not the tipis of the plains Indians. The Apaches and none of the southwestern Indians had the buffalo to furnish hides for covering the large tipis, and the availability of long poles was also a problem.

The Apaches made small, low wickiups instead.

These were bent sticks or brush that were tied together forming a shelter maybe four feet high and curving down on the sides. The framework might be made of any material, inch-thick brush and sticks, or more likely in the desert, the long and dead branches of the ocotillo cactus.

The framework might be strong and heavy with branches nearly touching, or it might be a simple skeleton. Over the frame would be put some kind of covering. Sod on the strong ones, twisted grass, branches, perhaps an old army blanket or frayed and tattered buffalo robe taken long before.

Morgan made it to the biggest wickiup before anyone challenged him. He saw only one warrior step from another wickiup and stare at him in shocked surprise.

Morgan stood outside the wickiup and bellowed out a cry of welcome.

"Good morning, Chiricahuas! It's a great morning to be alive! I come to talk to your chief!" He said all of this in English, and when a surprised Indian head popped out of the big wickiup, Morgan signed, "welcome" and "friend" and then asked to see the chief of the band all by signs.

The head vanished. Two warriors ran up from other wickiups and stood staring at Morgan, a white man unarmed suddenly appearing in the midst of their secret camp. The fighting warriors hadn't even brought a weapon.

A moment later the chief of the Chiricahua band stepped from his wickiup, his breechclout in place, his feather in his hair, and a look of astonishment still on his face.

"I am Morgan," the white man signed. "I come with important news about the Pony Soldiers who are near and searching for you."

Common courtesy required the chief to respond.

He did in sign so fast Morgan had trouble following it.

"I am Lone Eagle, leader of this band. You say Pony Soldiers are near? We have not seen them."

"You have no lookouts or scouts. I sent a friend ahead to warn you, Gimpy, did he arrive?"

A look of surprise again washed over the chief's face. He gave a quick, curt order and the two warriors who had first arrived hurried off toward where Gimpy had been tied.

"He came, we did not believe his rantings. He is safe."

"We must talk. Someone left an easy to read trail to your camp. A child could find you here. You must send warriors to brush out all signs that show movement into the canyon that leads to the secret entrance to the valley. The Pony Soldiers have good scouts."

"Where are Pony Soldiers?"

"Less than six miles from here. One hour of Chiricahua trot. The soldiers hide in a canyon to the north."

Again the chief gave orders and two more men hurried away. By now there were at least 25 warriors behind Morgan watching the small drama play out.

"You are White Eye, why do you come warn us?"

"I have seen enough killing. I have many friends among the People. I am tired of war. It is time for the long talk."

"We have left the worthless reservation. We go to Mexico."

"I have brought a present for you," Morgan signed. He held out the gunbelt with his favorite .45 Colt in the leather and 20 rounds in the loops.

"Short gun?"

"Shoots six times." Morgan held up his fingers.

The chief stepped forward and Morgan handed the belt to him. By this time in their warfare against the whites, most Indians had learned to shoot rifles, but to some revolvers were still strange. Morgan showed him how to cock the hammer before firing. The leader of the band cocked the hammer and aimed at the sky and fired. He smiled and waved Morgan into his wickiup.

A small shiver of excitement slanted through Morgan. Acceptance. The chief, at least for the moment, had accepted his story. Inside the wickiup, Morgan had to bend over. He waited a moment for the chief, then sat down near a small cooking fire. The entire length of the shelter was no more than ten feet.

The chief sat in front of a small fire.

"Coffee," the chief said motioning to a small metal pot on the fire. He signed that he had learned to drink it at the Agency and now had it whenever he could.

"How many Pony Soldiers?" Lone Eagle signed.

"Two hands, fifteen times," Morgan signed.

Lone Eagle frowned. "Many."

"You have women and children here?" Morgan asked.

Lone Eagle nodded. A small woman came and moved the pot holding the coffee. She poured it into two china cups and the leader smiled.

"Civilized cups," he said in English.

Morgan grinned. "It is good," he said in English and Chief Lone Eagle nodded.

They drank the coffee and said little. Morgan knew that the chief was waiting for a report from the scouts he had sent to some high point to check on the story about Pony Soldiers.

When the coffee was gone, Lone Eagle looked up. "You must be tired after your journey," he signed.

This was another stall until the chief found out whether Morgan was telling the truth.

"That is true," Morgan signed.

"You spoke of killing. Recent killing?"

Morgan decided in a moment. The chief must know about the attack on the Blue River.

"The Pony Soldiers came from the Blue River where they destroyed a camp. Only a few warriors escaped."

Lone Eagle looked grim for a moment. "They came here," he signed. "Cousins."

"I'm sorry."

"I'll show you a place to rest," Lone Eagle signed. They went outside to a smaller wickiup down the stream and the chief talked a moment to a woman at the doorway.

"This is Mitena. She lost her husband in a raid into Mexico last year, she will care for you."

The woman could be about 25, it was hard to tell. She was slender, small and now ducked her face in embarrassment.

"Where is Gimpy, the one I sent ahead to talk to you?"

"He was afraid, we thought he was an enemy. He is resting."

"Thank you," Morgan said. The woman motioned for him to go inside and he ducked and entered. The first thing he saw was a sleeping pallet built slightly off the floor and covered with a buffalo robe, much worn, and two army blankets. He didn't want to know where they got them.

Then he remembered that the reservation Indians were issued army blankets when they went to one of the camps.

He settled down on the blankets and looked at the wickiup. It was dusky inside. Then Mitena opened the entrance flap to let in more light. It was a well built shelter, with many cross members in the frame. He hadn't noticed what was covering the roof.

These shelters were built on the camp site and left when they moved on. In the southwest the Indians often needed little or no shelter except in the worst of the winter.

The woman knelt in front of him and signed. "Do you wish food?"

"Yes, if you have enough," he signed.

"Here we have plenty," she said with her hand motions.

He watched her quickly blow a coal into a fire around small twigs and sticks. Then she put a small metal pot over the cooking fire and emptied something into it from a pottery bowl. She added some water and then looked up at him as she heated the food. He had no idea what it might be. Certainly not flapjacks, sausage and a pair of eggs.

"You are the first White Eye I have ever seen," she signed.

"Am I so different?"

She laughed softly. "Not what I can see." She looked down quickly after signing it.

It was his turn to laugh and her eyes danced as she watched him. "It is good to laugh," she signed.

She looked down quickly and took him the food. She gave him a wooden spoon and when he looked in the bowl he found baked beans mixed with some small bits of meat of some kind.

"Beans?" he signed.

"We grow them when we have time here," she signed.

He tried a spoonful and found them good. Not enough salt to his taste. He grinned. He was staying alive on beans, not playing the gourmet diner. He ate the rest of the beans and she brought him a gourd filled with water. He drank it. She took the bowl and gourd away and sat beside him on the pallet.

"What is your name?" she signed.

"Morgan," he said out loud. "You are Mitena." She nodded.

"Morgun," she said. He nodded.

"I have not been with a man since my husband died. Now it is my honor to be with you." She slowly unbuttoned the reservation issue man's shirt she wore, and then let it fall off her shoulders to the pallet. She lifted her breasts. "I am without child. Would you give me child?"

She caught Morgan's hands and brought them up to her small breasts.

"*Por favor*," she said in Spanish. Morgan had forgotten that many of the Apaches were quite fluent in Spanish since most had lived in Mexico part of their lives.

Morgan fondled her breasts, feeling his hot blood rising. Then she moved his hands and pulled his mouth down to one of her orbs. Her hands moved to his crotch where she found his erection starting to rise. Mitena grunted in pleasure and tried to get inside his fly. At last she found the buttons and opened them.

Her hands found him and she gave a small squeal of delight. Morgan moved to her other breast realizing how similar this young Indian girl was to a white girl. Just a small shade of skin color separated them.

Mitena moved on her back below him and pulled him over her. The reservation skirt she wore came upward as her legs parted and he saw she wore nothing below the simple skirt.

She struggled to get his erection out of his pants and Morgan watched her in delight.

A voice came sharply at them from outside. It stopped the girl and she pushed him aside and sat up reaching for her shirt.

"Lone Eagle wants to see you," Mitena signed. "Come back, I need you," she finished signing. Morgan checked his fly, fastened two buttons and then moved out of the wickiup. He straightened as he emerged and saw a warrior there waiting for him. He motioned forward and Morgan followed the Chiricahua.

Lone Eagle sat in the shade of some brushy trees next to the chattering little stream. He held a knife and carved on a war club handle. The wood was dark, and it showed three different colors depending on the depth of the carving.

"Your carving is good," Morgan signed.

The chief waved the idea aside. "It is as you said, many Pony Soldiers are camped five to six miles away." He signed it. The chief went on carving. "We saw their cooking fires, and their scouts."

The leader of the Chiricahua band lay down the carving and threw a stone into the stream.

"White Eye who signs like an Apache, you were right. The trail in here could have been followed by a ten year old White Eye. I have sent 20 warriors to brush out all signs of our movement from a half mile beyond the valley entrance between the small hills."

"The Pony Soldiers will search for you tomorrow," Morgan signed. "You must have out scouts."

Morgan stood and looked toward the far end of the little valley. "Is there a way out upstream, an escape path?" he signed.

"No. This is a trap. If the Pony Soldiers find it, we all die or surrender."

Morgan sat down and threw three stones into the

stream at slow intervals. He had to think. At last he looked at the chief.

"You must lead the Pony Soldiers away from your people. Give them a trail to follow. Eight or ten men came this way from the Blue River. Send eight or ten out leaving a trail. Head back toward the west, northwest, then after fifteen miles, have the warriors split up and leave no trail at all as they circle back to this stronghold."

The chief said nothing. He threw a rock into the stream. Morgan watched him but remained silent.

After five minutes, the chief picked up his stick and began to carve again. It was thinking-work for the chief, Morgan decided. He stretched out on the bank determined not to cloud the Indian's thinking with any comment.

Morgan almost dozed off. It was nearly a half hour later before the chief put down the war axe handle and looked at Morgan.

"You think like a Chiricahua. It is a good plan. If the Pony Soldiers do not follow the trail, we will have to move quickly to Mexico. There is no place here that we can be safe. You have done my band a great service. Lone Eagle does not forget his friends."

He made a motion with his hand and Gimpy walked up to the stream. He stared at Lone Eagle a moment, said something rapidly in his native tongue and then sighed.

"I am undamaged, but I hurt," Gimpy signed. He sat and touched the cool water.

"You both have the freedom of our camp," Lone Eagle signed, then stood, took his carving stick and walked away.

"I thank you for my life," Gimpy said softly in English.

"There was nothing else I could do."

"You do not feel bad turning against the Pony Soldiers?"

"No, there has been enough killing. I mean that. An even fight, man to man is one thing. Slaughtering a whole people is not right."

Morgan tossed one more stone in the water. "How are you feeling? I saw how they lashed you to that pole. I couldn't get to you last night."

"No blame. I'm stretched out. I'll be fine in two days."

"You have a wickiup?"

"No, they said I could sleep under the trees. They gave me a reservation blanket."

Morgan told Gimpy about the plan to lay a false trail to lead the Pony Soldiers away and then let it peter out halfway back to Fort Thomas.

"It will work. Then we will live with the Chiricahuas for a time. Everything changes, everything remains the same. An old Coyotero saying."

Morgan stood. "I've got to go. You get yourself well. We might need to make a dash out of here, you can't tell."

"Say hello to Mitena for me," Gimpy signed. "She will keep your bed warm tonight."

Morgan nodded. "This afternoon as well as tonight," Morgan said and hurried back toward the wickiup.

Chapter Ten

Morgan had a long drink at the creek, then went to the wickiup where Mitena lived. He saw that the roof was made of long grasses covered with dirt and then a thin layer of stones to hold it all down.

"Mitena?" he called at the door.

"Sí," she said in Spanish from inside.

Morgan pushed aside the blanket that covered the doorway and slipped in. At first the difference in the light was so severe that he could hardly see. Then his eyes adjusted and he saw the young Indian girl sitting on the pallet where they had been before.

She wore the same clothes, but the shirt was unbuttoned and one of her hands caressed a small perky breast.

Morgan slipped down beside her, replaced her hand with his on her breast and nuzzled his lips against her neck, then licked her ear.

Mitena made soft noises deep in her throat and pushed against him. He felt the heat of her body through their light clothing. Her breast almost burned in his hand. He caught the other one and he felt that both nipples were hard, already raised from petting. Her skin glowed with heat and he helped her slip out of the shirt.

"Oh, *sí, sí!*" she said.

The words came over and over again as she stripped off Morgan's shirt and laughed and played with his dark chest hair. He kept caressing her breasts and her heat built and built. At last she went up on her knees and pushed down her skirt and kicked it off so she lay naked before him, her arms over her head, her thighs parted wide and her knees up.

She jumped up in a minute and worked on his trousers, opening his belt and the buttons and stripping them off him.

Mitena cooed and whimpered when she saw his erection spring up from his clothes.

"Oh, *sí, sí, sí!*" she said again. This time she dropped on his crotch, her hand holding his shaft as she pulled it into her mouth.

"Hey, you don't have to do that," he said, hardly realizing he was speaking English.

She didn't hear him. Mitena bobbed up and down on him, one hand fondling his scrotum and fingering his balls until he thought he would go out of his mind. His hips picked up a motion and then countered the movement of her head.

Morgan wondered how long it had been since he'd had a woman. Long before Phoenix. He couldn't afford one and he never paid for loving anyway. He was in no condition to seduce anyone.

"Oh, Lordy!" he breathed. She had worked one hand around to his bung and pushed a finger into his anus.

"Sweet mother of Mary Ronkowski!" Morgan

rumbled. Then he was panting so hard he couldn't talk. He pumped harder and she measured him and bounced back. The great flood gates opened and Morgan felt the total ecstasy that is like nothing else in the world. The only feeling he ever had that he wished would never end.

His hips jerked again and again and she took all he had and left him only when he pulled her up beside him. He was still panting. He felt vulnerable, as if a small boy could strangle him to death. He gripped the woman and she responded, muttering and murmuring not words exactly but a sound that soothed and relaxed him. Soon he slept.

She brushed her lips across his cheek and he awoke. She had done a fantastic job on him. He almost never went to sleep afterwards.

He moved and she was alert, watching him from dark eyes, a pleased smile on her face. She left the pallet and brought back a pottery bowl filled with cool water. She bathed his face and torso with the cold water, and blew on his skin to cool it as the moisture evaporated.

Then she dried him off tenderly. When she put down the cloth she sat her naked little bottom astride his chest and hung one breast down to his mouth. The orb glowed with a sheen of sweat from her labors. He licked it clean, then nibbled on her nipples until she moaned in rapture.

Morgan lifted her hips, straightened out her legs and lowered her so her crotch met his. She reached down and lifted his once again fully erect shaft and positioned it in her slot. Slowly Morgan let her down as he lanced into her and she shrilled a cry of pain and pleasure.

They lay there locked together, Mitena panting, her eyes wide, her breasts crushed against his chest, her little bottom poked in the air and starting to move in a slow, grinding circle.

"Oh, damn," Morgan said.

She laughed and lifted up on him and dropped down, lifted and dropped, then worked higher on him and her motion took on more a forward and back direction.

A few strokes later she was riding him bareback like an Indian pony, romping and riding along, panting and moaning and when she felt her own climax coming, she shrieked so loud half the camp heard her.

Mitena didn't care. She whooped again and then stiffened and rattled and shook and vibrated like a wooden trestle with a fast train going over it. She bellowed out her delight and humped him harder and harder until there was one huge last explosion and she dropped on top of him spent and sounding like a steam train taking on a fresh supply of air.

Morgan's own satisfaction was lost among her various peaks of joy and now he held her as she came slowly back to earth. She moved and looked up at him.

"*Es bueno*?" she asked.

"Yes, Mitena, *sí, muy bueno.* Best I've had in weeks, maybe months. You're going to make my stay here a lot easier than I thought it might be. Now let's hope that those ten braves can create a trail that the calvary will decide to follow."

That was when he realized the Pony Soldiers had no real scout left. He slid away from the girl and pulled on his clothes. He had to tell Lone Eagle to have the warriors make the trail so easy to follow that even a second lieutenant could find it.

He found the leader of the band near the river talking with two other warriors.

Morgan signed that he had something important to say, and the chief nodded.

"The Pony Soldiers have no scouts," Morgan signed. "Make the trail from here toward Fort Thomas so easy a blind man could follow it."

"It will be done," Lone Eagle signed, and Morgan nodded and walked away. When he got back to the wickiup, Mitena was in front waiting for him. She motioned to him and signed that they should walk up the stream.

Morgan wanted to see where the water came from and what the top part of the small valley looked like. It was no more than 200 yards long as he had guessed, and the top of it was a green swatch of grass and brush and trees where it was well watered.

He guessed there must be 20 or 30 springs coming directly out of the rocks or out of the ground in front of the nearly verticle rock wall at the top of the valley. There was no place to go but up. It was a true box canyon on both ends.

They sat beside the water and then Mitena waded in lifting her skirt. Morgan had not put on boots and he stretched his feet into the water. The dark eyed girl splashed him, and Morgan splashed her back. A moment later they were laughing and shrieking and having a water fight that soon resulted in their becoming soaking wet and sitting in the six-inch deep water.

Morgan couldn't remember when he had laughed so much. Before they began to shiver in the chilly water, they got out and lay on the green grass in the hot sunshine to dry off. No one came near them.

Mitena watched him carefully and brushed the wet hair back out of his eyes. She caught his chin and stared at him.

"Morgun," she said, then signed: "Please make me a baby now."

He pointed to the spot where they lay. She shook

her head, jumping up and ran behind some green brush. He followed her there and she lay on her back. Morgan planted his seed deep into her fertile womb. It was good.

By the time they got back to the main part of the camp, Morgan had counted the wickiups. There were only 12 of them. The rest of the men and some whole families lived in small lean-tos built under the trees. He guessed there were about 30 families here, perhaps five more. They would all be slaughtered if Major Phelps found them.

Back at the council fire they saw three women getting the fire ready to light. There would be another council tonight. The lookouts would report, the men from the trail planting group would be back.

Mitena pulled his hand and they went back to her wickiup. There she fixed food for him. There were potatoes. Morgan looked at them in surprise.

"Potatoes," he signed.

She nodded. "We learned to raise potatoes and beans in the reservation. The warriors refused to plant, but the woman dig for roots and collect nuts and berries. We learn to plant the potatoes and beans and when we left, we brought seed with us in case we found a place." It was a long signing.

By the time it was done, Mitena had coated four potatoes in a wet clay and rolled them into the coals of the cooking fire. They would be done in about a half hour, Morgan figured. He had done the same thing once in Idaho.

A neighbor brought Mitena half a rabbit and she thanked the woman, then set about roasting the meat over the fire which she built a little higher. This time she had coffee, which Lone Eagle had brought to her.

An hour later, Morgan settled back on the pallet

and watched the small woman cleaning up after their meal. It had been good. But he knew the Chiricahuas would not eat this well every day. The potatoes and beans must be a Godsend to them. He wondered if they had been here for some months.

"Almost a year," Mitena signed. "We plant more beans and potatoes whether we will be here or not. If not, they seed and grow more until we come and harvest."

She caught his hand. "Council," she signed, and they hurried out of the wickiup. Morgan was asked to come and sit near the council, but not with them. Mitena sat with the women farther away. Gimpy came beside Morgan.

"You and woman make wild time today," Gimpy signed. "Everyone in camp heard her."

Morgan laughed. "After a year, you would make a lot of noise, too," Morgan signed back.

The council was to report on the try to lure the cavalry Pony Soldiers away from the valley.

The 10 warriors who had made the trail told what they had done and how far they went. Gimpy translated the words with signs and Morgan caught most of it. Now all they could do was wait.

The lookouts reported that the Pony Soldiers were getting ready to move. There had been small patrols out toward the valley, and some in the other direction. The lookouts thought that the whole group would be riding the next morning.

After the council, Morgan was called to talk with the leader of the band. Gimpy went along. They settled near the big fire and enjoyed the warmth in the chill of the mountain night.

"You were scout with Pony Soldiers, Morgan," Lone Eagle signed. "Why did you warn us about the soldiers?"

"I am tired of the killing. There is too much. The

White Eyes have no right to kill a whole people. Our way of life is not the same, but still we should be able to learn to live together."

Morgan began to sign it, but Gimpy translated. It was much faster.

Lone Eagle listened, and nodded. "It is good. Tomorrow we will know if the Pony Soldiers take the false trail. I pray to the spirits that they do. If they find us, many will die. My men will not surrender and go back to the San Carlos reservation."

"Is there enough food here to live year round?" Morgan asked.

"Yes, with the beans and potatoes," Lone Eagle said and Gimpy translated. "Chiricahuas digger Indians. I never thought I would see the day. With a few squirrels and rabbits and now and then a fox and coyote, we make do. Early this year we had a swarm of grasshoppers that were a good addition to our food."

"More seeds," Morgan said. "You could raise a dozen more vegetables here. Chickens. You should have White Eye chickens for eggs and fresh meat."

Lone Eagle nodded. "I have seen these White Eye pheasants you call chickens. Meat and eggs. It is good. But we did not have time to collect more seeds, or chickens, when we left. We left in big hurry."

"Will you go to Mexico, even if Pony Soldiers take the fake trail?" Morgan asked.

"Yes, before the cold weather. There are places there to see, raids to make, Mexican soldiers to chase."

"But you will return here next summer?"

"It is possible. Who knows?"

Morgan and Gimpy said good night to the band's leader and walked into the darkness.

"A lot different tonight than last night when we came here," Morgan said. Gimpy nodded.

Mitena joined them. She was shy around Gimpy. Morgan introduced her and she stayed close beside Morgan.

"Let's get up early in the morning and go with the lookouts to see what Major Phelps does with his troops tomorrow," Morgan said.

Gimpy nodded his agreement and went toward the woods and his bedroll.

In the wickiup, the small fire made the only light. They sat on the bed and Mitena reached for him.

"Una mas," she said softly in Spanish.

Morgan grinned. "Once more? Don't you think I'll wear out or get tired?"

She shook her head at him, not really understanding. She undressed him again and they lay on the bed. Then she scrambled naked from the bed and built up the fire more so she could see. She sat and stared at his naked form.

"Muy bueno, bueno, bueno," she said and Morgan laughed.

"Little Indian maid, you are something. I've never known any female who wanted to make love more than you do. I know that if you get pregnant, then it will be easier to find a husband, even as a second or third wife."

She put her finger over his lips and pulled him over on top of her.

"Little angel, you're going to wear me down to a nub," Morgan said.

He thought about it for a moment, shook his head and reached for her.

Chapter Eleven

Morgan was up and went with the change of lookouts. The two Chiricahuas were pleased that he was going along, and excited when he showed them he could sign. They were full of all sorts of questions. None of them had ever seen a White Eye close up before.

Morgan decided that meant they hadn't seen one they hadn't killed. The two lookouts and Morgan went down the short valley, through the slot in the mountain, and then climbed upward directly after going out the concealed entry.

It was a hard climb, hand over hand in places, and along a narrow ledge in others. At last, they came to a spot high on the mountain where they could look out to the north and south for more than 20 miles in each direction.

There was a slight ground haze that morning, but as the sun hit the area it burned off.

By the time they arrived at the spot and relieved

the other two guards, it was just after six a.m. Morgan pointed to the spot where the cavalry should be but they were not there. The other scouts had seen nothing so far this morning and heard no bugles or any movement.

Morgan searched down the draw that the three troops had been camped in and breathed a sigh of relief. They were moving and were only now coming into view as the gully petered out onto the surface of the plains floor.

Two men rode out in front, scouts of a sort. Probably someone from the troops who had done some scouting before, or some tracking. They must have found the trail by this time from their other patrols.

The first scouts they sent out, Gimpy and Morgan, had not returned, so Phelps was going to see what he could find on his own.

Morgan wondered what the officer would do once he checked the fresh tracks, the ones moving away from the mountains and toward Fort Thomas. It would be interesting.

The column was fully visible now and moved at a walk directly toward the first entryway into the mountain.

"They find no tracks there," one of the Chiricahuas signed.

Morgan nodded. "Nor in the next opening," Morgan signed.

It took the troopers more than a half hour to get to where the pair of scouts had stopped. A lone rider went out from the troop and conferred with the scouts.

"Probably the chief deciding about the tracks," Morgan signed.

The Indians watched, fascinated at the formation of men, the discipline, the control they had over the soldiers. It was something they never had seen nor experienced in their years of fighting as Indians.

Morgan watched as a rider he was certain was Major Phelps rode back along the tracks toward the mountains. He and the two scouts came to a point where the tracks evidently just began. Everything else had been brushed out.

The origination of the tracks was between the two slices of entryways into the mountains, so neither could be suspect. The soldiers came to the trail and one of the scouts stopped them.

Phelps evidently gave some orders. Two details of six men each broke off the main group and one scout galloped with each group to the two openings in the granite walls of the mountains to see if there were any connecting tracks there.

"Now we see how well your people brushed out the tracks," Morgan signed. The two scouts nodded.

Fifteen minutes after the patrols edged into the openings of the two small valleys into the hills, the troopers rode back. They talked with the leader, then returned to the troop.

Soon the detachment turned and followed the two scouts who moved away to the northwest on the fake trail the Apache Chiricahuas had laid.

Morgan cheered. "Your men did well," Morgan signed. The lookouts nodded and smiles showed. Their wives and families were safe for at least the time being.

Morgan waited to be sure the troops continued on the same trail. The other two lookouts had also stayed to find out what the army did. They would report to Lone Eagle when they got back.

When the troopers were nearly hidden by a swirl of dust far into the plains, Morgan stood from where he had been sitting on a rock. "Let's go back to the green valley," he signed. The two scouts who had been there all night nodded and led the way back down the mountain.

The news was received with great relief and shouts of joy and screaming and wailing of the women who had lost warriors in recent fighting, for now there would be no more need for the wailing and beating of breasts of any new widows.

Lone Eagle declared a celebration, a victory feast and dance. Morgan watched as the Chiricahuas prepared. These people were not used to the good life. They subsisted in a harsh and unfriendly domain. It was where they had been pushed by larger and stronger and perhaps tougher Indian tribes 200 years ago.

Over time they had thrived only by learning how to adapt to their rugged environment. The Comanche lived by the horse. They used them well, sweeping 300 miles across the plains to make raids and carry off captives. They bartered with horses, horses were used to buy a wife. A Comanche's wealth was in his horses. Some chiefs and leaders of bands might have 200 horses.

The Apaches, Morgan knew, had little use for horses. He had heard that an Apache might as quickly eat a horse as ride it. In this land where there was almost no grass or graze for horses, they simply could not become an important part of the Indian's life.

The Apache's used dogs for transport long after other tribes had switched to horses. Morgan had seen Lone Eagle's horses. He had only five in the whole band. All were used to drag travois when they moved. Usually the horses would be stick figures, but here in the lush valley they were fat and sleek. Once the band moved on toward Mexico, the horses would lose weight dramatically.

Morgan had learned a lot about the Apache way

of life. Since it was so rugged, the men especially had to be prepared. Small Apache boys were drilled continuously in the twin virtues of an Apache: cunning and toughness. These were the two major strengths of the tribes. Small warriors were taught that trickery ranked far above pure courage. In this point, the Apache was unique in the Indian world where courage was usually the top ranked attribute.

An Apache warrior who could silently, secretly and quickly make off with six horses or cattle from a ranch was much more honored than a warrior who stole the whole herd but lost two warriors dead in the raid.

Young Apache boys were made to stay awake for long hours at a time so they could learn how to deal with and overcome exhaustion. That was why Apaches could continue to run or walk through the blistering desert heat long after the cavalry's horses and soldiers dropped from the race.

The youngsters were trained as long distance runners. One of the tests for a young warrior was to run four miles over rugged country holding a mouthful of water. He was not allowed to swallow it or spit it out.

Morgan heard that an adult Apache warrior had to be able to run 70 miles in a day over the most formidable territory.

For the boys' final training, they fought with other young boys using slings and rocks and bows and arrows with dull points. To survive, the young boys had to rely on a shield made of leather and their agility at dodging. No wonder the Apache were so hard to tack down.

Morgan watched the preparations for the feast. He decided there were more people here than he first figured. There must be close to 50, with some

20 warriors.

Three men were sent out to another canyon deeper in the hills where they had found a colony of desert hogs. The creatures weighed about 20 pounds and they harvested them carefully so there were enough left to reproduce.

The hunters came back with two males and the pigs were butchered and set to roast over fires.

For the Apaches it was a great feast. Three kinds of meat, pig, rabbit and a coyote; potatoes fixed four different ways; beans cooked; beans cold in a kind of salad with fresh sprigs of water plants from the upper springs; some acorn mush loaf that had been cooked, then fried in a treasured skillet.

One woman had saved the sack of acorns from their last trip to Mexico two years ago. She had kept them for a special occasion.

There were only two drums in the camp. Apaches did not do much dancing, except to petition the spirits. But tonight they would dance to the drums until all but two men remained dancing.

It was an endurance dance and sometimes lasted all night and into the day. The drummers were changed often, but the men could not be touched or touch each other.

At the feast they spread out the food on reservation blankets under the shade of the trees well before dark. Morgan used a tin plate from the reservation and sampled the pork, and rabbit, then filled up on potatoes and beans cooked with squirrel. Lone Eagle brought him a cup of coffee. No one else in the band liked the White Eye brew.

Morgan talked with the chief by signing. "You will stay here? Everything you need is here. What more could you want?"

The chief smiled. "You do not know the Chiricahua."

Gimpy came up and quickly translated into English. He hesitated sometimes, but his English was nearly perfect.

"All my life I have earned my food by raiding in Mexico and in New Mexico and now Arizona," the chief went on. "My blood boils when I do not get to go on raids. My best days are when I am sneaking up on some unsuspecting ranch and taking a dozen cattle right out from under their noses.

"We Apache do not make coup. We do not take scalps. We do not kill except in defense of our own lives, or to pay back an enemy who has killed some of our people. We live to make raids. How can you ask me to stay in this box canyon? It is like a large well watered grave. It is as bad here as at the reservation if I can't go on raids."

"How much longer will you stay here?"

"Perhaps one more full moon. We have been here more than a year. Our people and our horses grow fat. We are not used to so much food, such easy living. We grow soft."

Lone Eagle smiled. "Our older people like it. They say stay a while more, we can hurt and go hungry any time. Stay a short time more.

"I am not an old woman. I am Chiricahua. I live to raid. We will stay one more moon, then leave for Mexico."

After the food was gone, the women cleared away the things left while the men went to the council fire area and readied it for the dance. The rock fire circle was moved to the middle of a large flat place, and a new fire started.

Then the drummers, took their positions and began a slow beat. Soon the men jumped into the flat place and began dancing around the fire. The rhythm was slow and steady. After five minutes there were more than 25 men circling the fire. By then, the women had also come to the dance. A few began stepping into the circle as it moved around the fire from left to right like a slowly grinding human chain. No one touched anyone else.

Mitena came and sat beside Morgan, watched him, then pulled him up and to the dance. He protested but she would not be denied. She showed him the simple slap steps they were using. That seemed to be the constant with the dancers doing anything they wanted with the rest of their bodies.

Morgan looked in surprise as he saw three young women dancing with their breasts uncovered.

Mitena signed to Morgan that any unmarried woman who wanted to could dance that way to show herself off to prospective husbands.

Morgan stayed with the dance for a dozen circles, then slipped away and sat on the grass watching. After another dozen rounds Mitena left the dance and sat beside him.

"Two of the young women showing their breasts are no longer dancing," she signed to Morgan. "They are courting."

She stood. It was dark by now, the fire flickered on the bodies moving around and around the dance fire. Suddenly the beat picked up and the dancers shouted their approval.

Mitena caught his hand and pointed to her wickiup. Morgan grinned and headed that way. He realized they hadn't made love at all that day. It would be a busy night.

The next morning Mitena took his hand and they called on the man who had shot the coyote. Mitena bargained with him, and at last promised him a whole jack rabbit, unskinned, for the coyote hide.

The hide had already been stretched inside out and the excess fat and tissue had been carefully scraped off. Now it was ready for drying and tanning.

Mitena took the hide and traded it to an old woman who had no wickiup. She traded for a quarter of a cowhide the woman had brought with her from the reservation. The old woman would make warm mittens from the coyote skin.

Mitena laughed as she hurried back to her wickiup.

"Now I make you proper moccasins," she said. She found the thinnest part of the cowhide where the tanned leather was soft and more pliable than the tough, thick part. She had Morgan put his bare foot on the leather and she traced around it with a long piece of charcoal.

Then she waved him outside and she went to work with her knife and awl and sturdy leather thongs. In an hour she had a pair of moccasins made. They fit perfectly.

Morgan admired the moccasins, then looked at his pants. He took out his knife and cut off the pants legs above his knees, and discarded his shirt. But he kept his hat. The hat gave him protection for his head. Slowly, day by day now, he started to look more like an Apache.

He had a talk with Gimpy. The little red man had found a widow he was romancing. She had no one to hunt for her. Gimpy was satisfied to stay a while.

"When they move south into Mexico, I'll be heading back to the reservation and the army," Gimpy said. "I can tell them the band captured both of us and I escaped, and that they boiled your brains out over a slow fire. I'll get my scouting job back. Phelps is still going to be mad."

Morgan sat near the creek and took his moccasins off and dangled his feet in the cool water.

"Lone Eagle is right, this is no place for a warrior. I guess I'm a warrior. Raise some vegetables, hunt for a little meat, first thing you know you get soft. I guess I'll be leaving, too, when they head south. Maybe I'll go along with them to the border. Wilcox, Arizona, is down that way. I might stop in at that little town and see if I'm still a Wanted man in Tombstone.''

"Sounds dangerous."

"No more than living with a Chiricahua for a month." They both laughed softly.

"Is Mitena taking care of you?" Gimpy asked in English.

"She feeds me well, made me some new moccasins, and is wearing my pecker down to a nub."

Gimpy chuckled. "I figured."

"So we just sit here a while. In a couple of days, Major Phelps will be back at Fort Thomas mad as a roasted rabbit. Not much he can do but march his unit back to San Carlos and regroup. He'll have one big victory to report to Washington."

"You not go back to army as scout?"

"Hell, no! I was out of work, only reason I signed on. Hell, I'll find something. I can always work my way back to Idaho and see if my horse ranch is still there.''

"Good. I hear tell the young men are asking for an *O-kee-pa* ritual."

Morgan looked up. "Be damned! I've heard of them. Never seen one. You figure we're Chiricahua enough to watch?"

Gimpy stared at him. "You know what *O-kee-pa* is?"

"Not exactly. Some kind of physical torture endurance test. The young bucks pass it and then they go on to be warriors. Thought that was a Cheyenne ritual. How the hell it get way down here?"

"Might not be the same," Gimpy said. "But enough the same. The Coyoteros don't use it."

"Just what kind of physical pain is involved?" Morgan asked.

"They make two slices through the skin on your back up near your shoulders, and lift the skin and push a sharp stick a half inch thick through the two cuts so the skin is holding in the stick. Then they tie rawhide to the ends of each stick and hoist up the body so it hangs from the two points of flesh on your back."

"Damn! That hurts just thinking about it." Morgan shook his head. "How long they stay that way?"

"Fifteen maybe twenty minutes," Gimpy said. "No sound is permitted from the one suspended. Then to increase pain they tie a 15 pound weight on the man's feet. Cheyenne use a buffalo head."

Morgan lifted his feet from the water. "Forget it. I might not want to watch."

Gimpy shook his head. "You won't get to watch. Not you. Warriors want to thank you for saving their camp. They will talk to the council tonight about letting you be honored and undergo the *O-kee-pa* ritual yourself."

Morgan stared at him and his mouth dropped open in stark amazement.

Chapter Twelve

Morgan couldn't believe what he had just heard. "Gimpy what do you mean the council will talk about me undergoing the torture of the *O-kee-pa* ritual? I'm not Chiricahua. Hell, tell them no thanks, I'd rather not have that honor."

Gimpy shook his head. "It is an honor that no warrior from another tribe could refuse. It is an honor that is almost never awarded anyone not of this band. It would be a terrible insult to the entire band if you were permitted by the warriors to do *O-kee-pa* but refused. There would be no kind feelings for you at all."

Morgan scowled. "Hell, I didn't ask for the honor."

"No matter, it may be offered."

"If I refuse to do the torture, I'll be booted out of the valley?"

"Yes, perhaps without one hand, perhaps with only one foot, maybe without your hair. A great honor such as this, when refused, can turn into hatred quickly."

Morgan pounded the ground with his hand. "Damnit. Maybe they'll offer you the ritual."

Gimpy shook his head. "They know I am Coyotero. Our two groups have never been friendly."

Morgan slammed his hand into the ground again, then lifted his feet from the cold water of the stream so they could dry in the warm sun.

"Maybe no problem," Gimpy said.

It was just after midday when three Chiricahua warriors found Morgan and Gimpy. They signed that the council wished to speak with Morgan. He stood, gave Gimpy a murderous smile, and followed the delegation back to the council fire. There was no fire, but the elders sat around in the same place.

Gimpy went along with them to translate, if needed.

The warriors ushered Morgan to the center of the council and provided a small mat woven of straw for him to sit on. He faced the 25 warriors of the band.

"It is time to show our great appreciation to our friend and fellow warrior, Fighting Hawk. This new name we give you and welcome you to the Chiricahua band of Lone Eagle."

Morgan stood and bowed to the group, then signed. "I am honored to have a Chiricahua name. I accept it with pleasure and pride. No greater gift could Lone Eagle present to me."

Lone Eagle nodded, pleased. "We only return some of the respect and honor due you for service to our band. We are well aware of your bravery and skills. We do not question these, nor judge you. It is with pride and joy that we designate you a special friend and provide for you a private ceremony to welcome you into our band of warriors."

The chief continued to sign. "Today you will join us in a celebration of the *O-kee-pa* ritual, making you a lifetime Chiricahua forever honored by all Apache bands, and respected by all bands of the People everywhere."

Morgan had known what was coming. He had been arguing with himself, trying to figure out how to escape this torture honor and still retain his scalp and both hands.

Morgan tried. He signed. "I am honored and touched greatly. But I do not deserve this tribute. I am not of the Chiricahua blood or of any Apache blood. I am only White Eye. I have not had the rigorous training of a Chiricahua youth. I cannot run for even four miles with a mouthful of water."

Some of the warriors smiled and nodded.

"Nor can I trot through the desert, hills and ravines for 70 miles in a day and be ready to fight. I am not worthy of this great honor."

The warriors looked at their leader. He whispered with several of them, then faced them and spoke softly to them so Gimpy could hear only snatches of it. For a moment there was a pause in the talk, then two of the warriors stood. Lone Eagle turned back, smiling toward Morgan.

"The council has spoken. All but two have deemed you more than worthy of this great honor. The ceremony will begin in an hour."

Two warriors hurried up beside Morgan and signed that he should follow them.

"Now is the time to say no," Gimpy said softly in English. Morgan knew it. He couldn't take the chance. How hard could this be if 15 year old boys could stand the pain? He would do it. He had little choice if he wanted to ride out of here a whole man.

He squared his shoulders and walked between

the two much shorter Chiricahua warriors. They went to the edge of the camp to a wickiup and one man ducked inside. He came out with a breechclout, a small shield made of hard leather and an Indian bow and three arrows.

One of the warriors indicated to Morgan that he should take off his pants and put on the breechclout. He did so at once, curious just how it was worn. This one turned out to be little more than a long piece of cloth that wrapped around his crotch, around each leg and around his waist.

Curiously it held his genitals securely in place and it felt quite comfortable.

The Chiricahuas never used war paint or fancy feather headdresses in ceremonies or when fighting as the Plains Indians did. They couldn't afford the luxury of the wasted time and a big show in battle was not their forte.

There was a saying the soldiers had used at the fort. "You never see a Chiricahua until two seconds before he kills you."

But for this ritual, the most sacred and important in the tribal life, the initiate had his face dabbed with three colors and long lines painted on his body.

On his face went red, stark white and green. Morgan hoped that they would wash off. Stripes of red and green circled his body.

When he was properly painted, he was given a gourd containing water and told to drink all of it. He had an idea he would need it before the ritual was over.

With the Mandans, where the ritual originated, they performed it in their large oval permanent dwellings that had been constructed from logs and then curved thatched and dirt covered roofs. These buildings might be 15 feet tall in the center.

Other Plains Indians used the largest tipi

available. But the Chiricahua had no such dwelling, so they used a convenient tree. The comparison with being hung from a sturdy oak flashed through Morgan's mind. He tried to forget it.

By the time Morgan was prepared and walked to the largest tree along the small stream, the entire village had arrived and sat around to see the ritual. Morgan carried the shield on one arm. There was a leather loop in the back where he put his arm through and that was enough to hold the shield to his arm. In his other hand he carried the short Chiricahua bow and three arrows.

Now he saw that all of the warriors had dabs of the white paint on their faces. Some were nearly covered. These were the older warriors. Others had only one or two dabs.

Already a braided rawhide rope had been thrown over a tall, strong branch. At the lower end of it, the rope had been braided in four pieces. Three feet up from the end of the rope it was split into two sections so each could be tied to the skewers through his back skin. Morgan thought about it for a minute. He remembered how he had pushed a pin into his skin through the part that didn't hurt. Maybe this would be similar.

The people who watched, about 50 he guessed, did not make a sound. A drummer began a slow beat and one of the oldest warriors sat behind a round rock with a flat top. A war axe with a metal blade lay on the rock. What was that for, Morgan wondered?

Then two more warriors came up to him and escorted him to the spot under the rope. One signed to him that he should be ready, they would cut his skin in back. "Do not make a sound, no cry of pain, or we all will lose face," the warrior signed.

Morgan steeled himself but had to gasp in

surprise when the knife cut through his skin and lifted it. Then another slice and he could picture the cuts two-inches apart, each two-inches long.

He sucked in a big mouthful of air through clenched teeth as the green pointed stick drove under his skin through one cut and out the other one. Now he could feel someone tying the rope to the skewer. They looped it around both ends of the stick so it couldn't slip off, then re-tied it to the rope above.

Morgan grimaced at the pain as the other shoulder was done. Now he knew what to expect and it hurt even more. But he couldn't let out a single sound of pain. If the damned 15-year old kids could do it, he could.

That was the general idea.

A moment later, the second rope was tied off and they brought out a wooden box three feet high. The two warriors asked him through signs to step on top of the box. So far there was no pressure from the ropes on his back but the cut skin hurt like fire.

He stepped up on the box, and now he felt the rawhide rope pulled tight over the branch above. He looked and saw the rope tied off around the trunk of the tree much the way he had seen hangings done.

The pressure on the skin of his back was now enough to make him gasp. A shiver went through him and then a long sing-song voice began. It must have been in Apache language. It was an entreatment of the spirits, the rain spirit and the animal spirits of the rabbit, the mountain lion and the deer.

Slowly the pressure on Morgan's back increased. His skin bellowed out messages of pain. Morgan looked down and saw four warriors slowly sliding the wooden box out from under his feet. It was done gradually, so there was no sudden drop. The braided rawhide rope stretched as they all did, and the pressure increased on his back. The skin held as it eased away from his flesh.

The rawhide rope held.

The skewers held.

Then he felt his feet drift free of the wood.

Morgan sensed more absolute physical pain than he had ever thought possible. Wave after wave of pain seared through his shoulders and back. The original hurt of the cutting of his skin was now washed away in the agony of the continuing pressure of the stretched skin and the pain sensors.

He tried to think of good things, of good times. From the position of the skewers about four inches down his back, he hung with his shoulders slightly forward and his head down. Any attempt to lift his head was murderous. He stared at his feet for a minute, then saw the shield on his left arm. That reminded him he had to keep holding fast to the bow and three arrows. His hand cramped for a moment, then relaxed and he held onto them.

How long, oh god, how long? Morgan thought. He had heard once that most of the participants fainted after 15 to 20 minutes.

The pain flooded through him again and his mouth came open. He almost dropped the bow but caught it as it slipped. Agony! He had never felt anything like it. Continuous, like holding your hand in a fire, or like a bullet ripping into your shoulder every second.

The good times! Remember the good times. The pleasure of the small Indian woman last night. The good times.

He felt himself turning slowly. A warrior used his lance and turned him slowly so all could see him. He closed his eyes again.

The good times. Remember the good times!

The first time he rode a horse. That had been wonderful. The thrill of riding by himself, of having a little control over the full sized beast. Then the first horse he ever broke. How he was thrown four times, but got out of the dust and convinced the stallion that the man on his back was the boss. Oh, yes, there had been a lot of good times.

Damn the pain!

For a minute he wanted to bellow out his frustration and pain and agony, and scream to be cut down and let them heap their abuse on him.

Then he opened his eyes and stared directly at a boy no more than 12 or 13 watching him, fascinated, eyes gleaming, as if he were waiting only for the day when he could prove that he, too, was brave enough to be a Chiricahua warrior.

Morgan bit his lip. He tasted the blood. He sucked on it and closed his eyes again as he turned slowly. For a moment he thought he would faint. Then he grabbed his consciousness with a strong grip and held on to it. He opened his eyes as far as he could and watched those in the crowd.

He saw Gimpy. He was squatting on the grass as if suffering part of the pain. On around the circle, Morgan spotted Mitena. Her face was flushed with crying. Tears rolled down her cheeks as she watched. Then his gaze locked with hers and he tried to smile, but couldn't. She smiled and nodded and grinned at him and then he turned on around.

Morgan knew he shouldn't rotate his head. He let his head hang straight down and looked at whatever came in his view. The pain built now, built higher and higher. When he opened his eyes, for a moment all he saw was blackness. Then slowly the light came through again.

Sweat dripped into his eyes. He couldn't lift his arms to wipe it away. Even moving his arm slightly doubled the pain in his back. Morgan blinked to get rid of the moisture, but it didn't work.

The salty fluid touched his eyes and stung.

He felt the blackness coming again. Morgan held onto the bow and arrows so tightly that his hand ached.

The blackness slid away and he could see again. He relaxed his hand on the bow and arrows but didn't drop them.

How long? He wanted to scream, but he was permitted no sounds of any kind. Damnit! When would it end? At least they hadn't tied a buffalo skull to his feet.

How long had it been? A minute or ten minutes? He couldn't tell.

The people watching turned around in front of him again. This time they were moving, he was hanging still. The waves of pain were less now, maybe he was getting numb, or passing out. He tried to open his eyes, but he was too tired. His hands at his sides seemed like sticks.

Did he still have the bow and arrow? He'd have to do it all over again. No! He still had the bow and arrows. He could feel them in his right hand which was cramping.

Movement, he felt movement. Probably someone pushing him again. The blackness came in drifting waves now, in and out. He opened his eyes once and could see everything, then the ground seemed closer. Couldn't be.

He moved again, a little slippage, like the rope over the branch slipped. Again. Then again. Morgan forced his eyes to open. He willed them to come unglued and for his eyelids to swing apart.

At last they did. He stared at the ground. Now it seemed so close, maybe inches away. Couldn't be. The pain drilled through him again and he opened his mouth to scream. He'd had all he could stand. Any man reaches a breaking point.

But 15 year old kids could do this and never whimper.

Hell, he wasn't 15 any more.

He was about to scream his lungs out when his feet touched something. He looked down.

THE GROUND!

All the saints be praised! His feet hit the ground and it was solid, but his knees wouldn't hold him up. They bent and someone lowered him again until he was sitting down.

Eager hands grabbed him. It was over. At least the first part was over. What was the next part? Another wave of blackness surged toward him and he opened his eyes wide and battered it back, back, back until he could see Mitena with tears on her cheeks, but she was smiling.

Chapter Thirteen

It was not over.

Two warriors lifted him as they untied the ropes and quickly jerked the skewers out of his back. He felt a new rush of pain and it brought back the agony of minutes before.

Then the braves led him over to the man sitting beside the rock with the war axe on it. They sat him in front of the stone and took his left hand and extended the little finger over the top of the rock.

Morgan was so groggy he wasn't sure what was happening. He saw the elder warrior lift the war axe, aim it carefully and then swing it down toward his finger. At the last moment the warrior with the axe angled it away from his finger so it struck the stone and a great cheer went up from the Chiricahuas.

"Much brave, no chop off finger," one of the Chiricahua men signed.

Morgan understood, at least he thought he understood. They took him away from the stone and pointed, then signed that he was now expected to run around in a circle outlined in rocks. Morgan stared at them, blinked back the darkness again and signed asking if they wanted him to run the circle. The two men beside him nodded.

They let go of his shoulders then and he took a small step forward just to catch his balance, then another step and in a moment he was doing the Chiricahua jog around the circle. For the first dozen steps he was trying to maintain his upright position. He nearly fell with each step. He was afraid his knees would buckle again.

He made it all the way around. A cheer went up from the watchers. He made another circle, then when he looked down at the rocks there were two of everything.

He shook his head and looked again, still everything he saw was double. Morgan tried to keep running. He went between the rocks he saw but stepped on one and staggered. A sudden sheet of blackness slammed down around him and he stopped.

As quickly as the blackness came it vanished. Now he could see normally and he continued to jog around the circle. Did his back still hurt? Was he bleeding? He didn't know about the blood, but the tremendous reduction in pain on his back meant he couldn't feel any pain there.

He staggered. He was tired. So tired. His steps went slower on the next circle. Now the pain came again, gushing, surging at him. It seemed to center in his head, not his back. Slowly one eye dimmed until he saw everything in gray black shapes. Then the other eye went dim and he stumbled and fell into a black void that he was sure had no bottom.

When Morgan awoke, he was back in the wickiup. A cool, wet cloth covered his forehead and Mitena cradled his head in her lap. She smiled down at him as he looked up.

"Most brave," she signed.

Morgan groaned.

"You'll live now," Gimpy said. He stared down at Morgan for a minute, grinned and went out the wickiup door.

Morgan moved one arm and his back, shoulder and side hurt like someone had stabbed him with a cactus.

"Stay still," the girl signed.

"Yeah, stay still and sleep and maybe eat something," he said. But before he could think any more about that, he slid back into sleep.

It was two days before he had recovered enough to feel human again. Mitena had tended to his back. She used some of the same green poultice that Gimpy had used on his chest.

"Healing," she signed. "But must leave scars."

"Why scars?" Morgan signed.

"To show all that you are *O-kee-pa* Chiricahua. that you are blood brother, that you are worthy of pain."

"That's going to mean a hell of a lot in some fancy upper class bedroom in Denver or St. Louis," he said out loud.

Mitena looked at him questioningly, but he shook his head.

Gimpy came up to the front of the wickiup and called out.

"Come on in, Gimpy, we're just talking about social values."

Gimpy bent down and edged into the shelter.

"Big doings. Council. Let's go listen."

He signed it so the girl would know. The three

of them went toward the council fire area, and Mitena stayed back as the two men went forward so they could hear.

Gimpy listened for a few minutes, then scowled. "We're moving. The great chief Geronimo has sent a message for all Apache to gather in Mexico to prepare for one great fight against the White Eyes."

"How long will they stay here?" Morgan asked.

"Not sure. They are still talking about it. They don't need to be in Mexico for two moons. Some want to stay here another month. Others want to move down slowly, striking at the small ranches and crossroad settlements along the way."

"Sounds like it's serious."

"Damn serious, but we can't make out like it's our business."

"Hope they stay a week or so," Morgan said. "I'm not up to a long hike through the desert."

"Which way will you go?" Gimpy asked.

"I ain't about to go to Mexico. How far is it to the nearest White Eye settlement?"

"Army stopped at a little crossroad place called Safford a year ago. Don't know if it still there."

"How far?"

"Twenty-five miles, maybe more. Due west."

"An afternoon's stroll. We better plan on heading there if we can get clean away from here."

"You are now blood brother Chiricahua. You can leave any time you want."

"And you, Gimpy?"

"I am Coyotero, not bound by Chiricahua."

"I'll need four days to a week to get back to full fighting trim," Morgan said.

Gimpy listened to the talk of the council again. He shrugged. "We don't have much time. In two weeks the camp will move out with everything packed on the six travois, heading south."

Morgan scowled.

Gimpy listened again. He stood and motioned Morgan away. "The runner from Geronimo said that this must be the year of the blood. The army has killed many Apaches. Now Apaches will show the White Eye what war is like. The year of blood. Kill all whites that can be found."

Morgan walked along the stream. "Then this will not be a peaceful raiding trip to Mexico. This band and every other will leave a trail of blood wherever it goes."

"Sounds like it. The army would like to know about this," Gimpy said.

"Your job. You're still on the payroll." Morgan stood looking into the small creek. "How far are we from the border?"

"Maybe 100 miles," Gimpy said.

"How many villages, towns and ranches between here and there?"

"Twenty, twenty-five that they might hit before they get to the Coronado Mountains, then down the back side to the border."

"That's what I was afraid of. This time the Chiricahua aren't going to steal horses and cattle and women and slip away. This time Geronimo has called for blood. They'll leave a trail of death down the side of the territory. How can I let them do that? I'll have to think about it."

"Think well, friend," Gimpy said. He wandered off toward the place under the trees where his woman waited for him.

Morgan walked back to the wickiup and Mitena followed. She had heard. She watched Morgan inside the wickiup for a moment, then she pulled down the reservation blanket and reached for him.

"I heard about the move," she signed. They said nothing more.

Morgan figured she knew that he would be going in the other direction. He had to make the Chiricahuas think he was going back to the army, back to the north, away from their route.

Then he thought no more of it. The small woman worked out of the soft reservation dress and sat before him in the faint light naked and working on his pants. He had not worn a shirt since his *O-kee-pa*.

She played with his chest hair as she always did. None of the Indians had chest hair and few had any whiskers to count. His chest hair had fascinated her since the first day.

Morgan fondled her breasts, watching each one surge and heat up to his touch. Then the small pink nipples slowly rose and filled with hot blood and pulsated so strongly he could feel her heartbeat.

She worked his pants down and off and then removed his short underwear and gave a small cry of joy and pleasure when she found him already hard. She kissed his tool and then gently found his balls and rubbed them and played with them until he moved her hands.

She lay down on the reservation blanket and held out her arms for him. Morgan spread over her, careful not to let his weight crush the small figure.

"Morgun," she said and he kissed her.

He wasn't sure if Apaches kissed or not but she responded and her hands found his hardness between them. She stroked him.

Her small body turned into a hot, burning, writhing form below him as her intensity built up and up until he thought she might explode. His hand pushed between them and found her small clit which he struck a half dozen times.

Mitena humped her round bottom upward as the first spasms shot through her. She whimpered like a dove as the vibrations shook her and a long moan came from her mouth as she tapered off and put her arms around his neck.

She lifted him and guided him as his stiff pole found a place to fit into.

Mitena gave a small cry of joy and satisfaction as he drove into her gently until their bodies were locked together so tightly neither one of them could move without moving the other.

"Is good," she said in English.

Morgan looked at her, surprised.

"Gimpy?" he asked.

She nodded and then began to grind her hips around and around. The motion always got to him quickly and now, almost before he thought possible, the gates opened and he blasted forward eight times. He sent his seed jolting into her fertile field.

She pushed her legs upward until she could lock them around his torso and she smiled at him.

"Stay" she signed. "Best for making babies."

Morgan eased down on her a little but still holding most of his weight on his elbows and his knees.

After what Morgan guessed was ten minues, she patted him on the shoulder and unlocked her ankles.

They sat up and she signed. "You go away?"

He signed back. "Lone Eagle band go to Mexico soon."

"You go with us?"

"I don't know. Much to think about."

"You Chiricahua now."

"Just my back," he signed and she laughed.

He touched her flat little belly. "We want Chiricahua baby in there," he signed.

Tears seeped out of her eyes and she caught at him. "You ready to make baby again?" she signed.

He laughed and told her in a few minutes. "Food first," he signed.

She got up and started a fire in the fire ring and boiled potatoes. He had shown her how to peel them first and then mash them and she was fascinated.

Mitena cooked half a rabbit over the open fire until it was juicy and well done on the outside, but temptingly pink inside. She boiled coffee the way he had shown her and Morgan settled down to a satisfying supper.

They finished eating and made love again slowly and softly that brought small, delicate whimpers from Mitena as she lay perfectly still. Her mother had told her this would help the roots of the baby to find its way into her womb.

She roused after five minutes and watched him. Suddenly she smiled and reached up and kissed him where he hung over her.

"We made baby today!" she signed.

"How do you know?"

"I know. I am now a mother! Baby growing!"

Someone spoke outside the closed curtain of the wickiup. Mitena looked up and pushed him away. She said something in response. The man outside talked again.

"Lone Eagle wants to see you at his wickiup," Mitena signed to him.

"Must be important," Morgan signed. He pulled on his pants and slipped into the moccasins she had made for him. He bent and kissed her cheek.

"I'll be back, little mother," he signed.

She smiled and waved as he left, then her hands went down to her belly and she patted the tight flesh gently.

Morgan left the wickiup and saw the warrior waiting for him. He walked at once to the largest wickiup. There was a bright fire burning inside. The escort pointed to the open door of the wickiup and Morgan bent down and shuffled inside.

This shelter was larger, with a bed along each side and one across the rear. Near the front and the smoke hole, sat the leader of the band, Lone Eagle. He nodded to Morgan and waved at a place near him in front of the fire.

Morgan sat there, cross legged. He stretched his back and could still feel twinges as the skin continued to heal together. The pain was less now, but he could still make it hurt.

He stared at the fire, then at the leader.

"You know we will be leaving this place soon," the Chief signed.

Morgan nodded.

"Will you be going with us?" the leader signed.

Morgan looked at the fire, then began signing. "Far to the north, past Colorado and Wyoming, as far as a Chiricahua can run in 15 days, there is a bright green, rainy land called Idaho. There I have a ranch where I raise horses. I was heading there when I took the short job as scout for the Pony Soldiers.

"Perhaps the spirits guided me to them to help protect your band from the blueshirts. I must return to my own wickiup in Idaho, to my green lands and to my horses."

"Fighting Hawk, you are now Chiricahua, you are free to come to our band or to leave whenever you wish. We will wish you well."

"How long will you stay here, Lone Eagle?"

"We will begin to prepare for the journey. We will hunt for rabbits and wolf and mountain lion and coyote to make dried meat. We will dig potatoes and slice them and dry them in the sun as we always do."

"We will harvest our dry beans but leave enough

of both to seed themselves again so they will be abundant when we return. We will be here for half a moon."

"I will stay until I feel fit enough to walk out to the White Eye village to the west. One hand of days. Gimpy will go with me, if it is all right?"

"He is Coyotero, he comes and goes as he pleases."

"We will help you get ready for your trip. Do you go all the way to Mexico?"

"Yes. to Mexico."

There was a pause and Morgan knew he should ask no more questions. He nodded at the leader, said a farewell and slipped out of the wickiup.

He had thrown the dice that carried the secret of his life or death. Only time would reveal how the dice turned up.

Chapter Fourteen

Morgan walked toward his wickiup and a shadow fell into step beside him.

"Heard the chief wanted to talk," Gimpy said.

"Indeed he did. He confirmed that they pull out in two weeks. I told him I wouldn't be going with the band, and he didn't seem upset. He said I was Chiricahua now, I could come and go as I pleased. Said we both could."

"So we walk out. When will you be ready, Fighting Hawk?"

Morgan grinned. "Another four or five days, a week at the most. Figure we can make that 25 miles in about eight hours, especially if we leave here about an hour before sunset."

"Sounds about right. I'll go get two rabbits we can dry in the sun and use for jerky. That and our canteens should be plenty."

They stopped and looked at each other, nodded and went to their separate sleeping quarters.

As soon as Morgan stepped into the wickiup, Mitena watched him in the soft firelight.

"Fighting Hawk, are you going with us to Mexico?"

He hadn't wanted to tell her yet, but now there was no way around it.

"I can't go with you," he signed. "I have a horse ranch in Idaho, 15 Chiricahua warriors running days to the north."

"Idaho," she said. Then she signed that she had heard the word earlier. She urged him down on the pallet beside her.

"Once every day we make baby," she signed. "Mitena must be sure."

"You'll wear me out so I won't be able to walk away from here," Morgan signed.

She nodded. "I hope." She smiled and patted her belly. "Tell me about White Eye world," she signed.

"What part?"

"Houses. I've seen houses. Why live in house?"

He told her all the benefits of living in a house, how it kept you dry when it rained, warm in the winter, how it kept out people you didn't want in, but that you couldn't take it from one place to another.

"I don't want a house," she signed. Mitena looked pensive and wrinkled her forehead. "Tell me about big village, town, city," she signed after a moment's thought.

He told her about the many houses, the streets, the boardwalks, the places where you could buy food and blankets and pots and pans and clothes.

She watched him sign. He spoke the English at the same time so she might pick up a word here and there. Mitena seemed thoroughly sold on cities.

"Why don't all Apaches go live in city?" she signed.

"You would scare the White Eyes, and you must have money to live in city. Money buys the things you want. White Eyes work hard all day for money. Then trade it for food and clothes."

"Money?" she signed.

"Money, currency, bills, gold coins."

"Gold?" she asked in English. He looked up startled.

"Yes, gold coins will buy things."

"I have gold coins," Mitena signed.

"Show me," he signed.

She worked under the pallet and brought out a leather bag with a draw string on the top. It was a foot long and half that wide and she untied the leather thong through the slits in the bag and opened it. She took out papers and an ink pen, and last came tumbling out a stack of gold double eagles.

Morgan picked them up and looked at them in the firelight. They were real. He put them back.

"Where did you get the gold?" he signed.

"My short time husband got it on a raid at a house. No one home, he go in house and find these things in bag and bring them. He was to make necklace for me from coins."

Morgan chuckled. "That would be an expensive necklace, and heavy," he signed.

Morgan took out the coins and stacked them in piles of ten. There were 40 of the coins—$800! This small woman had a fortune on her hands and didn't know it.

"Will you make me a necklace?" Mitena asked. "You make necklace for Mitena, you can take the rest and spend them in big city. Buy new clothes and food and horse."

She signed it all with a big smile and reached out and hugged him and nodded yes, hoping he would respond.

"Yes, I make you a necklace," Morgan said.

He picked up one of the papers and unfolded it. It was a stock certificate, a railroad stock from somewhere in Illinois. The stock was for 500 shares. He looked at the rest of the papers and spread them out in the firelight. There were more stock certificates, and bearer bonds with face values of $500 each.

"You like the pretty paper?" Mitena signed.

"Yes, it is pretty paper," Morgan signed.

"It is yours. You make Mitena baby and it is all yours."

Morgan looked at the stocks and the gold. A fortune to most men. There could be from $5,000 to maybe $20,000 here, depending on the stocks. There was no chance to find out who might have once owned it. One of the many Apache raids among the White Eyes. Impossible to locate the rightful owners.

He scratched his jaw in contemplation.

"This pretty paper can be traded for gold coins," he signed to her. "It is valuable."

"Not valuable to Mitena," she signed. "It is yours. Mitena want necklace of gold coins." She put down the paper and touched him. "First we make baby."

Whether from her mother's indoctrination, or Mitena's own innate urging, she insisted on lying on her back for the lovemaking. Tonight it was not passion or screeching, it was a planting ceremony and she did little but get him ready and then insist that he remain tied to her for ten minutes afterwards. All the time she chattered in her native language, and now and then signed to him that she was sure this was the time she would get pregnant.

Later, Morgan looked at the stock certificates. Some of the companies he had heard of. Others he hadn't. He was sure some of the stocks would be worthless. Companies went broke and bankrupt all the time.

Still, there could easily be $20,000 worth of paper there. She had given it to him. Hell, he should try to find the owner. Maybe the stocks were registered to some owner. Maybe.

He took out his knife and began boring holes in U.S. gold coins. He would use five of them. He needed some soft wire to space them apart. The nearest jewelry story would have it. Sure.

He got the twin holes bored in the top of the coins about half an inch apart so the wire or string could go in one side and out the other and keep then hanging flat.

He explained to Mitena what he needed, some kind of sinew for the string. She nodded and went to the back of the wickiup to a square willow woven box and rummaged around. Soon she came up with three pieces of sinew about a foot long.

"Taken from coyote gut," she explained by signing.

Morgan tested it and found the nearly clear, whitish material was strong. He made the holes slightly larger, then strung the coins on the sinew. They all folded and fell together.

Mitena looked at it and he explained he needed something to keep the coins apart, something stiff like trade beads. Mitena held up her hand, took a knife and hurried out into the darkness. It was only two or three minutes until she came back in carrying some willow branches. They were no larger than her small finger. She sat by the fire, cut them into pieces an inch long, then slit the sticks and carefully peeled the bark off them.

She held the inch long pieces of bark toward the fire and they curled into a circle about a third the size of the branch they had been on. She gave one to Morgan. He lifted his brows, then threaded the sinew through the hollow coil of bark and put a coin on each side. It worked.

Morgan kissed her cheek and told her to make five more of them. He used the four tightest rolled, tied two pieces of the gut together and soon had the necklace. Morgan hung it around her neck on her bare chest and asked her how low she wanted it to hang.

Mitena adjusted the height, and Morgan tied the sinew together in back. He covered the knot with a piece of the rolled up bark that would still unroll without breaking.

"It is beautiful!" Mitena signed. "I'll look at myself in the still pool of water tomorrow."

She would not take off the necklace as she lay down to sleep. Morgan knew she might crush the bark in the night, but she could make a new divider and put it on before the bark dried so it would roll around the sinew.

The next morning, Morgan went hunting with Gimpy. Other hunters were out as well. Gimpy shot three rabbits with a borrowed bow and arrows, divided one with Morgan to eat and they skinned the other two. They stripped off the meat from the rabbit bones and hung it on a pole fitted with small sharp pointed pegs. It would take three hot days of sun to dry the rabbit well enough to preserve it.

Morgan watched the women digging potatoes. They pulled the plant from the ground, dug the soil with flat sticks until they found all of the potatoes, then they replanted two at each hill so there would be more when they returned.

The dug potatoes were saved in straw baskets. Most would be stored that way and loaded on the travois. Some would be sliced and laid in the sun on clean rocks to dry.

Mitena was helping. She was put in charge of slicing the potatoes and drying them. She and three small girls watched over the rocks near the river. They chased away the birds that tried to steal the sliced food.

Morgan watched over his rack of drying meat nearby. Mitena proudly wore her necklace, and the other women admired it. Morgan said he could make another one to give to a woman friend. Mitena flew at him in mock anger.

"No! I am only one in the whole band who has one. I will use it to help attract a husband. When I am with child, I will be a good catch for a second wife. Some of our women have no children. It is sad for them and for their husbands."

For the next three days they worked at the digging, drying and hunting. Now rabbit meat and that of a coyote hung all around the camp drying in the hot sun.

After two days, Gimpy took down their dried rabbit and wrapped it in a straw basket he had made.

Morgan still had the canteen he had brought into the desert. He rinsed it out and checked it. It did not leak. Then he and Gimpy traced the route he had run that first night, and after hunting all afternoon, they found Gimpy's canteen. The two would be enough to get them to the San Simon River and then into Safford, Arizona Territory.

Morgan grew stronger every day. Gimpy had been watching his back cuts and said that the skin had shrunk back down to normal after being stretched in the *O-kee-pa* ceremony and was healing nicely. In two more days he would be ready to travel.

Gimpy said he was a little surprised that the Chiricahua would let them go now that they knew of their plans to raid to the south into Mexico. Then he shrugged.

"I am Coyotero, they would have to kill me to keep me from leaving. We are cousins, they won't do that. But you are White Eye, even if you do have the Chiricahua sign of the *O-kee-pa* on your back, you are still White Eye. A Coyotero chief in the same situation would be sure you went with the band, or that you could not tell anyone of the expected raids."

Morgan watched him closely. "Do you think once we start to leave, that Chiricahua warriors will make sure we don't get out of the canyon?"

"It is possible. It is the Apache way. We are not known for our kindness."

Morgan went to his bed that night wondering if the smiling Lone Eagle would be treacherous enough to ambush him and Gimpy as they went down the valley toward the slice through the mountains.

Mitena took his mind off that worry by rolling on top of him and smiling.

"We make baby tonight!" she said.

Morgan planted his seed as deep inside the small Indian girl as he could and then when she let him withdraw, he rolled away again wondering about the route out of the valley. There was only one way. Lone Eagle could work an ambush at the entrance to the slit through the mountains or just past the secret entrance on the other side. Either one would be highly effective and almost impossible to get out of alive.

The next morning, Gimpy and Morgan made their final preparations. Morgan had traded his traditional breechclout for his cut off trousers that Mitena had washed in the creek. He found the tan shirt he had worn and she washed it as well and dried it.

The camp itself was about halfway through with preparations. The had enough meat for a journey of three weeks, but sent their hunters out again. They would not kill any females with small ones, but the male rabbits were fair game.

The beans had been harvested, threshed out and put in straw baskets. There had been plenty of beans left and planted so there would be a continuing wild crop.

New baskets had to be fashioned and the older women worked at making the tightly woven baskets from willow and straw that grew in profusion along the stream.

Morgan and Gimpy went to see Lone Eagle that afternoon and told him they would be leaving in two days. The chief gave Morgan back his six-gun but kept two of the .45 rounds for good luck.

Morgan held the six-gun belt and gun and holster and for a moment he almost changed his plan. Then he smiled. "It has been good to live as a Chiricahua for these few weeks, Chief Lone Eagle," Morgan signed. "Now I must move on to my other life in the White Eye world."

The chief nodded. Morgan slid the six-inch sheath knife from his belt in its scabbard and held it out to the chief.

"Whenever you must use this, think of your friend, Fighting Hawk," Morgan said.

The chief's eyes gleamed with joy. Here was a tool he could well use, far better than a short gun.

"Go with the Chiricahua blessing," Chief Lone Eagle said. The two men rose and left the chief's wickiup.

On the way back to Morgan's shelter, Gimpy smiled.

"You fool the chief. Tell him we leave in two days,

but we leave early tonight just after dark, right?"

Morgan grinned. "Yes. I still have a bad feeling that the chief would feel much safer if we were either with him, or rotting in the Arizona sun somewhere waiting for the vultures to pick our bones."

"There is no chance to steal two horses," Gimpy said softly. "One warrior watches them all night and never sleeps."

"So, we'll be on our guard. An hour after dark we start down the valley. One of us on each side. If we find any guards waiting for us, we must dispatch them silently."

Gimpy nodded. They parted in the late afternoon sunshine and walked back to their women. There would be one more planting of the human seed, and then Morgan would be ready to go.

Chapter Fifteen

An hour after darkness, Mitena slept soundly on the pallet, a smile wreathing her face after making love. Morgan had not told her he was going tonight. He couldn't risk it. He picked up his gunbelt and strapped it on, pushed the packet of gold coins and stocks inside his shirt and lifted his canteen and the small package of dried rabbit.

He and Gimpy had agreed that each would go down the nearest side of the valley to where his sleeping place was. That would put one of them on each side. If they found any guard or ambush, they were to try to settle the problem quietly.

Morgan did not underestimate Chief Lone Eagle. If he knew Morgan was leaving tomorrow, he very well may have posted a lookout or two tonight, just to be safe.

Morgan moved to the far side of the valley away from the small stream and shifted from one dark spot of the green carpet to the next. The moon was a sliver but still gave off considerable light. Ahead of him he saw nothing unusual. He made it to the point where the stream switched sides of the valley, less than 20 yards from the entrance to the secret passage through the mountains. As he entered the woods, he thought he heard a long sigh ahead of him.

Morgan moved that way quickly and saw a knife glint in the moonlight and then descend into the chest of an Indian. Morgan rushed up with his boot knife out and ready.

Gimpy looked up as Morgan came within arm's length. Gimpy was the one using the knife. A Chiricahua guard lay on the ground dead.

Gimpy shrugged. "I saw him before he saw me, but he was dozing. I thought I could get past him without making a sound. I am not the Apache I once was. I had to silence him."

"Are there any more?"

"No. One would be all tonight."

They trotted to the opening in the wall and slid into it and stopped, listening intently.

Nothing.

They looked at each other, nodded and trotted down through the slice of a path between the slabs of rock. At the far end of the passage they slowed and came to the opening slowly, without a sound.

Gimpy went first, parted the scrub brush cautiously, stared all around. He moved like a feather through some of the growth, then came back.

"No one," he said. They went through the brush and into the harsher reality of the Arizona desert. At once they began their Indian trot that could cover six miles in an hour.

Morgan let Gimpy lead the way. From time to time the small Apache would glance at the stars, then ahead to the west. They trotted for an hour, and Gimpy slowed to a walk, then stopped. He motioned to the water and Morgan took a small drink.

The night was chilly as it usually is after dark on the desert. Morgan didn't know how cold it was, but it was a welcome relief after the heat of the day. He was not sweating much.

"We've covered about five miles," Gimpy said.

"If the guard was to be on until midnight, we should have at least a five hour headstart on them," Morgan said. "They won't be able to catch us."

"If we can average four miles an hour, we'll be 20 miles away from the valley by midnight," Gimpy said.

Morgan put away his canteen, checked to be sure that the gold and the stock certificates were still inside his shirt, and they started jogging to the west.

By midnight they were not 20 miles away, but they were 15. Morgan admitted that he wasn't as tough as the wiry Coyotero Apache.

Morgan heaved a sigh and sat on the sand as he tipped the canteen. "I know you're a better runner than I am, Gimpy. Sorry. How far away are we now?"

"Maybe 16 to 17 miles. Too far away for them to catch us. They won't try."

"Why not?"

"Cunning is a trait we Apache appreciate. You and I were sneaky and more cunning than Lone Eagle. He will nod and order his men to find out how long the Chiricahua guard had been dead. Then he will estimate our travel and call off a useless search. Instead he will leave quicker for the settlements to the south. That will be his sneaky response to our cunning."

"So we move again," Morgan said. He chewed on

the rabbit jerky for the next two miles, then had some more water and settled down to walking at their new speed of three miles to the hour.

At 3:30 a.m. they sighted the small settlement of Safford, Arizona Territory. They did not go in at once, but circled it watching for anything unusual. They found it on the far side. There was a fair sized encampment of military. Morgan counted three separate company streets with small pup tents set up in perfect alignment and order. It looked like the soldiers had been there for a while. A makeshift corral held what he guessed was 150 horses.

They looked at each other.

"Major Phelps?" Morgan asked Gimpy.

"Looks like it could be," Gimpy said. "I don't need to go to Fort Thomas."

"But I better make myself scarce," Morgan said. "I don't want to see the major again. Tell him we got captured, and that the Chiricahuas killed me. You are Coyotero so they accepted you. Then when you learned about their plans, you ran out of there."

"Should work," Gimpy said. "What will you do?"

"Hell, I can move lots faster than the major. I'll get some clothes, buy a horse and saddle and some food and take off by nine o'clock. You show up about then at the major's tent. I'll get down there and try to warn some of those ranches and towns between here and the border."

They parted. The army had camped on the edge of the little town near the Gila River, and Morgan walked a half mile upstream from the army and settled down in the brush near the water for some rest.

He woke up when a rooster on a nearby small ranch came alive with a salute to the dawn. Morgan stretched, figured it was about six and walked the half mile into town and roused the night man at the livery. He bought a fair horse for $50, paid another $10 for saddle and bridle and saddle blanket. Then he took the mount out for a get acquainted ride.

She was a chestnut mare with all four white stockings and a small white blaze on her forehead.

The animal rode easily, responded well, and was not skittish. Morgan stopped her in front of a small cafe that was open. For a moment the smell of all the food cooking and being served brought back a flood of memories. It had been well over a month since he'd tasted food like this.

He started off slow with an order of ham and eggs and fried potatoes. He polished them off with coffee, then had an order of hotcackes and sausage.

The waiter looked at him strangely.

"I'm hungry this morning," Morgan said.

He was at the general store when it opened. The owner looked at his cut off pants and nodded.

"Looks to me like some she bear caught you and got mostly pants," he said.

"About the size of it," Morgan said. He bought two pair of pants, another shirt and two blankets. Then he picked out a new hat, a wide brimmed Western style, low crowned in soft brown. Next he got a skillet and coffee pot and other camping gear and a supply of food for three days. He tied it all in the blankets, lashed it on behind his saddle and rode.

It was just after nine a.m.

He was almost at the edge of town when six cavalry troopers came toward him, with a sergeant in the lead. The non-com held up his hand and stopped the men. He walked up to Morgan's mount.

"Sir, we're looking for a man on foot with a brown shirt and cut off pants, named Morgan. Seen anybody like that around?"

Morgan shook his head. "He a desperate criminal,

or what?"

"Major wants to see him. He's a former scout we think is back in town. Thanks."

The troopers and their sergeant rode on into town. Morgan picked up his mount's pace to a lope and rode out of town due east until he hit the San Simon River, then turned south and made some time.

He stopped about noon under some trees along the stream that was growing smaller as he worked upriver. He saw no one. No settlements, no ranches. He might have to go all the way to the little spot called San Simon before he found people. It should be worth it.

The small community was at least 35 miles from the Lone Eagle Valley. With the travois, the Chiricahua could make no more than three miles an hour. A long day might put them close. Morgan didn't think that the Indians could be ready to move in two days. But they might. It was a bet he had made and the lives of those in San Simon were the chips.

By four o'clock he figured he had covered 26 or 27 miles. He would be in the small village before dark. He had been watching to the east as the mountains moved closer to the stream, but nowhere could he spot any dust trail in the silent and hot Arizona desert landscape. Through here six horses and travois and 40 or 50 Indians on foot would send up a continuing column of dust.

When he rode into San Simon an hour later, the small town was peaceful. It wasn't really a town. A dozen buildings clustered around the stream which brought life to everything nearby. There was a post office, a general store, one small saloon under a boarding house. No hotel, no livery stable, and only six or eight houses all within 50 yards.

He knew of one ranch nearby that worked cattle up and down the San Simon River, but he hadn't seen any cattle so far.

There was no sheriff here, no town marshal, no city police force, no mayor and no city council. Everyone looked out for everyone else.

He stopped at the general store. The owner was Paul Oso, and he watched curiously from the porch as Morgan rode up.

"Howdy, stranger. Offer you a beer?"

Morgan said that would be fine. They both settled down on the chairs in front of the store and sipped at the lukewarm bottled beer.

"Seen any Apaches lately?" Morgan asked.

Oso shook his head. He was a bear of a man, nearly six feet tall and thick at the waist. A blacksmith shed to one side testified to one sideline he worked at.

"Not a whimper. Have you?"

"Yep. Figure about 50 of them are heading this way. Geronimo has called for a year of blood. Means the Chiricahuas are going to be raiding and killing. Figured you'd want to know."

"How we know you ain't just fooling with us?" Oso asked.

Morgan stood up and took off his shirt, then turned around.

Oso was on his feet in a second.

"Christ! Heard about that. Never believed it was true. You went through that ritual O-kee something?"

"*O-kee-pa*. I did. I did them a favor and they didn't kill me. But I had to do the ritual. They have about 25 warriors who have rifles and bows."

Oso gave a whistle with his fingers between his teeth. A young man about 18 came out of the store.

"Yeah, pa?"

"Get out the word, Chiricahua gonna be here tonight or tomorrow. Everybody get their guns out and stay up. We'll be watching for them."

Morgan finished the beer and watched the small town come alive. Shutters went up on about half the windows in the houses and stores. They were inch thick planks to stop any arrows and slow down rifle bullets to a whimper.

"Better put your horse in my barn out back. It's got no windows. You figure they'll be here tonight."

"Not sure. Depends when they left the mountains." Morgan put his horse in a stall but left the saddle on her. Never could tell.

When he came back to the general store, Oso was handing out rifles and shells. There were 12 men there, and some boys 14 to 18. They all got rifles.

"Remember, lock the doors, board up the windows, and stay inside," Oso said. "Shoot from upstairs windows. Shoot at every shadow that moves cause you know none of us is gonna be out there to get scalped."

The general store owner looker around. "Any questions?"

"We gonna stay up all night?" a man asked.

"You want to stay alive, you damned well better," Oso said. The men drifted off and Morgan saw the rest of the first story windows having boards nailed over them from the outside.

"Done this before?" Morgan asked.

"Once or twice. Damn Apaches come through this way to get to Mexico. Last time they got four head of stock and two cows they butchered just outside of town, but they didn't kill anybody."

"This time it will be different, if they can do the job," Morgan said. "The more fight you put up, the quicker the Chiricahua will turn and try another town."

Oso tossed Morgan a rifle. "Noticed you didn't have one on your saddle. Bet you can shoot a little. Be pleased to have you in my upstairs window."

Morgan nodded. "What can it hurt? I was about to ask if you had any good sippin' whiskey that we could keep warm with up there."

Three hours later it was dark and Morgan and Oso sat beside an elbow level window on the second floor of the general store. They both had rifles and a stack of cartridges beside them.

A morning dove gave its "who whoing" call three times and Oso tensed.

"That's them. Somebody out near the edge of town has seen the damn Chiricahua. They're coming!"

Chapter Sixteen

Morgan sat in the second story of the general store in San Simon looking out the low window watching for the coming Chiricahua. He used his early training and sectioned off the danger area ahead of him, then studied each grid area at a time. He learned where the shadows were and remembered them. No one heard a thing. No shots had yet been fired.

For five minutes nothing happened. Then Morgan checked a grid that looked different. He concentrated on it and saw a shadow slowly grow larger. He sighted in on it and when it moved another inch, he fired.

An Apache scream of anger and pain jolted through the night. Guns went off from the street now and men in second story windows returned the fire.

Morgan found no other targets for the moment. Then a form rose up and threw a flaming torch.

Morgan sent two rounds into the figure that launched the burning brand. The thrower went over backwards and lay in the moonlight. The torch fell harmlessly on bare earth and burned itself out.

Morgan watched for someone to come and get the Indian. The Apaches almost never left a wounded or dead man for the enemy to desecrate.

A new shadow melted out of the old. Morgan watched it, was almost ready to fire, but waited a moment longer. In that blink of an eyelash, the Chiricahua grabbed a foot of the wounded or dead man and pulled him back out of sight.

"See any more?" Oso asked softly.

"Not yet. Are the barns protected?"

"We've got a man in each barn with a shotgun."

About then they heard the deep throated roar of a scattergun.

"That's discouraging even to an Indian trying to steal a horse," Morgan said.

They watched for another hour. No more shots were fired. No one tried to burn down a building. Everything was quiet.

After an hour of watching and waiting, Oso leaned out the window. "Anybody hurt or in trouble, sing out," he bellowed.

No one answered. "They must all be all right or all dead. Either way they don't need any help. We'll hold our positions until dawn.

"What about the other communities and ranches toward Mexico?" Morgan asked.

"Soon as you came I sent a rider each way," Oso said. "We got this kind of Apache Warning System all worked out. Anybody gets it or hears of the hostiles coming, we spread the word. The next place sends out another rider to the next town and so forth all the way to the border."

"You've been through this before," Morgan said.

"About a dozen times. A man gets to learn what to do."

A half hour later, Oso stood up. "You stay here. I'm going to check downstairs and see what else I can do. I'll send up a few more rounds for you just in case."

He vanished in the darkness and down the stairs. They squeaked as he went down.

A few minutes later the stairs squeaked again as someone came up. He caught the scent of lilac as a figure came toward him. A girl sat down beside him and handed him half a dozen cartridges. She let her hand linger over his as he took the rounds.

She settled down in the splash of moonlight that came in the window.

"Pa said I should bring you these," she whispered.

He saw the blonde hair falling over her shoulders, a softly rounded face that smiled.

"We don't get strangers here too often," she said. "Be all right with you if I stayed a spell and talked?"

"Sure, I'd like that. My name is Morgan."

"Howdy. I'm Beth Jane and this is my eighteenth birthday."

"Well, happy birthday, Beth Jane."

She nodded in the moonlight. "Usually I get a kiss on my birthday."

"Tradition is important," Morgan said. He reached over and met her lips. They trembled, then pushed hard against his and opened slightly. He put his arms around her and pulled her to him. Her mouth came open and invited him inside. He probed a moment, then came out and leaned back.

"That was nice, Morgan. But I'm eighteen, so you owe me seventeen more like that." She caught one of his hands and pulled it to her chest and he found she had opened the buttons on her blouse. There was no clothing under it. His hand closed around a breast and she pushed toward him and kissed him, catching his lower lip between her teeth. It was sometime before she let him go.

"Now, Morgan, that's just ever so much better." She held his shoulders and lay backwards on the floor, pulling him half on top of her.

"Won't your pa be coming back?" Morgan asked.

"Course not. That's why he sent me up with them shells. He wanted to say thank you from the town for the warning. We could have got several killed here otherwise."

"He's not coming back up?"

"Not till morning. He promised. You want to chew on my titties?"

Morgan rolled over so she was above him. "Drop one in my mouth and see," Morgan whispered.

She did. He chewed and that's when Morgan remembered he didn't have any supper.

"Hey, don't chew them off," Beth Jane whispered. "I might want to use them someday." She pulled away and slipped out of her blouse. That's when a shot fired outside.

Morgan pushed her aside and crawled over to the low window and looked out. A dark figure ran from between buildings with a torch. Morgan sighted in with the rifle and fired three times as fast as he could push new rounds into the single shot rifle. The last round brought down the figure with the torch still in the bare dirt in the middle of the street.

Morgan kept firing around the body. He made it impossible for anyone to retrieve it. Soon others found the target and from time to time fired near the prostrate body.

Beth Jane crowded next to him and watched where he shot. As he did she worked her hands up his legs to his crotch, then opened the buttons and found his erection.

"I just knew you wanted Beth Jane!" she said. Mogan fired near the body.

Beth Jane gave a little cry. She dropped down, opened her mouth and sucked in his hardness. She began working back and forth on it.

Morgan made a small groan of pleasure, then fired again.

Beth Jane gave a little cry and sucked and bobbed harder. She came off him and kissed his lips.

"When you fire that rifle it just gives me goose bumps!" she said. "I want you inside me."

"I was," Morgan said grinning at her.

"I mean in my hot little pussy!"

Morgan sat beside the window. "You figure out a way. I got to keep this rifle out the window." He fired again and reloaded.

Beth Jane moaned in anticipation. She got on her knees and snaked down her skirt and petticoats off her legs, then pulled off some thin underwear. Quickly she took off Morgan's boots, then his pants and underwear and pulled him out a little from the window where he sat.

She pushed his legs together and straddled him and inched her crotch up toward his.

"Hug me just a minute," she said. As he did she lifted and then lowered herself, guiding his stiff rod into her slot in a perfect match. She wound up sitting facing him, holding his sides with her hands.

"Oh, lordy! Jeeeeze is that wild. Shoot that damn Indian out the window!"

Morgan fired near the dead Chiricahua and Beth Jane crooned as she flashed into a grinding, shaking, shattering series of spasms that rocked through her body and made her tremble like an earthquake had hit.

Morgan grinned at her and looked out the window. He saw a shadow move some 20 feet down from the dead hostile. Morgan sighted in on it and watched. Slowly the form moved back deeper into a larger shadow cast by a farm wagon. Morgan waited.

Beth Jane recovered from her peak and began lifting and falling on his shaft. It was a strange angle and it excited him at once. He watched the shadow, then found that there were two of them moving gradually toward the dead man.

Morgan waited as they trailed along the sides of the wagon, enlarging the shadow by a foot on each perimeter. Then the wagon's shadow ended and they moved slower yet, extending it.

Morgan fired beside one of them and the hostile melted back into the darkness. The other Chiricahua remained still for two or three minutes and Morgan felt his own hips begin to work and his breath come in short gasps. The Indian moved.

Morgan fired, deliberately missing, kicking dirt in his face and driving him back to the shadows and he hoped down into the darkness between the buildings.

The moment Morgan fired the rifle that last time, his own gun went off blasting upward into the waiting vessel. That triggered Beth Jane again and she roared and panted and they fell to one side with her on top stretched out flat. Her hips pounded his, her breath surged in gasping pants until she shook herself to pieces. Then they both came down slowly until they could breathe again.

Morgan rolled over and slipped away from her. He looked out the window again. This time, nothing moved.

He kept watching out the window. An hour later, he pulled on his clothes. Dawn had begun to crack the mirror of night in the east. He finished dressing and saw that Beth Jane had awakened and watched him, shaking her bare breasts at him.

As it grew light slowly, he watched her dress. She was a bigger girl than he had at first thought, thick of the waist and with powerful arms and legs. A sturdy ranch girl. Her hair was blonde and long and her face prettier than he had hoped for.

She crawled across the floor to where he sat next to the window and kissed his cheek.

"You were wonderful last night," she said. "Better than I've ever had before. Much, much better. Wild, sitting up facing you! That was a first. Now I got to go help Ma get breakfast. Maybe we'll have time to play in the hay out in the barn before you go. When did you last roll around in the hay? It's wild."

She kissed his cheek again, patted his crotch and went down the stairs.

Morgan had been watching the light streaking across the sky. Now as it became strong enough, he checked where there should be two Chiricahua bodies. One had been pulled away, but the torch thrower was still there in the middle of the street. Morgan saw someone come out from a doorway and dart into the street and stare at the Indian.

Soon there were eight men and half a dozen women in the street. Morgan took the four rounds he had left along with the rifle and went down the stairs and out the front door.

He stared at the Chiricahua. Morgan was glad he didn't recognize him from the hidden valley. Typically, he wore no war paint and had no fancy feathers or headdress. The Apaches didn't use any of that. They just killed their enemies. All except this one.

Oso came out and took a count. No one was missing and only one man had been wounded. He was cut slightly on the arm by flying glass when a bullet came through his window.

"Two for us, none for them," Oso said. "They might go around us the next time they come this way."

Oso nodded at Morgan and they went into the general store and to the living quarters in back. Nothing was said about Beth Jane. She served the two men and the two grown sons breakfast. Morgan got three eggs sunny side up on four half-inch thick hot cakes, hot syrup, butter and a handful of crisp fried bacon. Coffee came in a bottomless cup. As soon as he drank from it, Beth Jane filled it. Nobody commented on it.

When the food was gone, they talked.

Oso grinned at Morgan. "You sure called the tune on them 'Paches. Got us ready in time. We're usually one of the first ones hit and we start the alert. We hurt them this time. I had Will ride out north along the river just before daylight. He says there's a big dust coming five or six miles out of town. Must be the army."

Morgan stood. "That means time for me to move. The army and me don't get on too good. I used to do some scouting for them. Don't mention I was here. Be obliged."

Before he could get to the door, Beth Jane came out with a bundle wrapped in a piece of bleached flour sack.

"Some sandwiches and a couple of apples," she said as they walked to the barn where his horse was. Once inside, she kissed him and bored into his mouth with her tongue.

He patted her breasts and stroked his hand between her eagerly parted legs.

"Darlin', like to get you all naked and hot again, but it's riding time. Next time I'm past here I'll say hello."

She had her hand inside his fly and stroked him, then pulled her hand away. "Morgan, you come back and we'll just go at it all day and all night for about a week!"

Morgan stepped into the saddle and rode out. They said the army was coming in on the west side of the river. He'd cross over and go out a quarter of a mile on the other side and should miss them completely. At least that sounded like a good idea.

Chapter Seventeen

Morgan rode in the brush along the eastern shore of the San Simon River downstream for a quarter of a mile, then came out and headed towards the distant mountains to the east. He figured he'd move out a mile from the stream. That should put him beyond any normal outriders of the army unit. Before he had his spot picked out, a rifle shot slammed over his head.

Morgan looked up and saw three blue shirted cavalry troopers moving in on him from three sides and another man 50 yards away with his mount stopped and his rifle aimed at Morgan.

"Hold up, sir," one of the troopers called.

The three rode up to him and one spoke. "The major wants to talk to anyone in this area inquiring of them about the movement of an Apache band."

Morgan snorted, nodded and rode back across the creek with them and jogged down to the main party of the unit that was coming forward. Morgan rode up to the man leading the first troop, Major Phelps.

"Morning, Major, how goes your war?"

Phelps looked up and scowled.

"Morgan, you son-of-a-bitch. You're supposed to be dead."

"That's what the Chiricahua think. You've got to be sneakier than the Apaches to beat them. You've figured that out by now. If you're looking for Lone Eagle and his band, he passed through here last night.

"The village was ready and reduced his number by two and didn't take any casualties. He's probably about 30 miles ahead of you by now. He's got six travois, 20 or so warriors and about thirty women and children. He can't travel more than three miles an hour, but he moves for 14 hours a day. You seen anything of Gimpy?"

A horse moved up and a grinning Gimpy waved.

"Hell, Gimpy, I figured that Chiricahuas forgot you were Coyotero and boiled you in a pot. How 'n hell did you get away?"

"You can discuss that later," the major barked. "Morgan, you've still under orders. Take the lead scout and put us back on Lone Eagle's trail."

"Not a chance, Major. One time facing a Chiricahua death fire is enough for me. I retired from scouting, especially against the Chiricahuas. Couple of dollars a day don't mean a damn·thing if your skull explodes over one of them small fires. You still got that buckskin I was riding? I'll trade you this fine, deep chested chestnut for her."

"You can't quit, Morgan. You signed on."

"True, now I'm signing off. Wasn't any time period on my duty. Now I'm through. Gimpy can find any Apache you want him to. Did he tell you about the year of blood that Geronimo has proclaimed?"

"Indeed he has."

"Believe it. Now, where the hell is that smooth riding buckskin?"

"You still have army property, Morgan," the major said.

"Just this canteen. You want it?"

The major shook his head. "All right, get along. See the sergeant back with the remuda. Tell him you can trade." The major watched Morgan a moment, shrugged and lifted his arm. When he swung it forward and down, the entire string of four abreast troopers began to ride ahead at a four mile an hour walk.

Morgan found the remuda and talked with the sergeant in charge of the dozen loose horses. Ten minutes later, Morgan had transferred his gear to the buckskin, waved at the sergeant and headed on downstream on the San Simon.

He was till nearly 50 miles from Safford, but he had two days of food left and Beth Jane's sandwiches. No problem. Once in Safford he'd rest up for a day or two, eat well, play a little poker and then find out if there was a stagecoach into San Carlos and on to Phoenix. He still had $700 in gold that would spend just fine, anywhere. He wanted to see how Jack Swilling's irrigation projects were coming along in Phoenix. He started them back in Sixty-Seven and the project seemed to be working. He'd heard that the small town of Phoenix was growing.

Morgan settled down to the job of riding another 50 miles through the rugged Arizona semi-desert. All he had to do was follow the San Simon River and he'd come out at Safford.

Two weeks later, Lee Morgan sat in an office in Denver. He'd been there three days, had bought himself two new suits of town clothes, including a fancy vest, a gold watch and a low crowned, wide brimmed hat that served well in the city or on the trail.

He watched an investment broker study the three issues of stock certificates he had shown the man. For a moment, the broker's bald head beaded with sweat, then he looked up and smiled.

"Yes, absolutely, these stocks are valid and currently listed by the New York Stock Exchange. I checked by telegraph last night as you asked me to. The current listed price is $13.27. There will be a two-percent sales commission."

Morgan nodded. "I understand. All right sell, I'll expect your check for the balance in the morning."

"If there's a buyer, Mr. Morgan."

"For this stock there is always a buyer."

Morgan left and checked his envelope. That was the last of the stocks and bonds. He stopped at a restaurant even though it was well before midday. He was met at the door by a uniformed greeter who took him to the dining room.

For a moment, Morgan relaxed. It felt good to have money again. It didn't bother him a whit that he was living off the labors and sweat of the brow of someone the Apaches had stolen from. Better Morgan using them than the stock certificates being burned up some day because Mitena grew weary of carrying them.

He consulted a bank book he now carried from the First Denver Bank. Tomorrow his new balance would read $39,770. He was in the money again. He could ride the train to Boise, or as close as he could get, and ride into town in style. If the sheriff had sold his ranch again, he would buy it back, run for sheriff himself and put an end once and for all to the clamor by that unscrupulous lawman to get the

Spade Bit Ranch out near Grove, Idaho.

Three tables over, Morgan had noticed a young lady watching him. She was not casual or hiding the fact. She stared quite openly at him and when he looked at her she smiled. Was it a trap or was she interested in him? He put down his menu and walked over to her table.

"There seems to be a crush here in the dining room this noon, Miss. I wonder if you would mind if I shared your table?"

She glanced up him and smiled, then looked around the dining room that had no more than ten people in it.

"Yes, there does seem to be a crowd. I'd be delighted if you could join me."

He sat down and held out his hand. "My name is Lee Morgan, and I'm from Idaho."

"How fascinating. I'm Lee Brothwick from Boston and this is my first trip west."

"Are you alone or traveling with a companion?"

"Oh, no, I always travel alone. I believe in seeing the country, learning about the customs and the people, and tasting life at its fullest."

"In that case, have you seen a Wild West Show yet? They are the rage here in Denver at the moment."

"That sounds exciting. Does the show present the West the way it really is at this time?"

"Not really. Nor is it as the West once was. But you'll see some real Indians, a lot of horses, maybe a live buffalo or two, and a lot of men and women riding horses."

"It sounds delightful."

A waiter came and they ordered.

After the meal she smiled at him. "When does the Wild West show start?"

"About two o'clock."

"Good," she said. He felt something along his leg. He realized she had slipped off a shoe and her stockinged toes were creeping along his inner thigh. "Perhaps after the show we can come back to my room and I can show you some of the etchings I've been buying on my tour."

"Etchings. That sounds delightful. Will you be in town long?"

"It depends, perhaps a week."

Morgan smiled. "That's about the time I'd planned to stay in Denver." He helped her out of her chair and she took his arm.

Yes, Denver for a week of good food, good wine, and a fine woman. Yes, he'd earned it out there in the Arizona desert.

As he led Lee toward the door, he had a fleeting thought that he couldn't push down. He wondered how Mitena was down there in Mexico. Lee Morgan knew he would never see or hear about her again. Still, a man can wonder.

"Lee, I think we better stop by my room before we go. I need to pick up some things."

Lee Morgan nodded. Now there was a good idea. If they didn't get to the Wild West show today, they could always go tomorrow.

Lee from Boston smiled a secret smile and caught his arm as they walked up to the second floor and to her room.